I0831970

Walking life
IN SIGNS

Ari Newhome

ISBN 978-82-998009-3-8

First published in Internet by Lulu.com

Viking LTD

A catalog record for this book is available from the Norwegian Library.

ISBN 978-82-998009-3-8

All text and photos are made by Ari Newhome

Preface: Walking Life in signs

Quite recently I was visiting Milan, in Italy. I visited an exhibition of some of the works of Leonardo da Vinci. They was really great nice details, he was a really great artist and a clever man. This book is not going to be about what he did, if you want that, you didn't buy this book, but I learned something from him, that I never will forget.

Leonardo da Vinci –

Don't learn this, you got your own sewing tools at home

That is one the greatest expressions I have learn in my life, and hope that I will remember that. He was an great artist, because he told me, if I am learning what he did, I will not be able to be creative.

This was a very great inspiration to make this book.

Expand you mind – beautifulness you will find

This is a story, just not like other stories, maybe a story about stories, Today i am going to tell you a very secret, a secret about secrets. It is about signs and dreams. As you already have noticed, this story started with "This" that is the first sign, just like a symbol. The rest of the story is about something, that is lost and we follow the two writers, Mr Dove and Peace, they are placed in a fiction story, on page 1. And as almost every book, they are just, blank in their heads, because they don't have a clue about what to do. As a famous reporter, I am going to talk to them, at the book signing. Just follow me, to the next line.

I walk up to them, and there are a lot of other reporters at the book signing, and I make my way to them into the crowd and asks

«How are you, buddies ? I just asking them, with my microphone up in their nose

«We are just, blank! Dove says

«It, doesn't seems so, you are flashing. I say

«What? Says Peace, with a questioning face.

«You guys are flashing white of all the lights of the photographers around.

«Hey, Peace, you are totally white, Dove says with a big smile

Peace laughs, and points with his right hand at Dove, and says

«You are to, Dove, with a smiling face

«We are lightened up, we got a sign, from heaven, they both replies, and it starts to rain dollar bills with, a strange sign, a pyramid

«We are rich, they both laughs, rich writers

«I am just going back to my wife and tell her, replies Dove

«Party poooooper, replies Peace, and continues with, this is it, what every writer wants, famous, signing dollars bills

«My wife told me to get, home after work, we are going to study some signs, she is expert on that, with her clairvoyants gift

«Ok, see you tomorrow, says Peace

Together they are dancing away in the rain of dollar bills, and singing an old Beatles song called:

"Working together", while the flashes of the cameras dies out.....

As a world famous reporter I continue my story, with following the signs of secrets. I pick up a book, that is falling down from the sky. I am looking up in the sky, and wondering where that book come from. The only thing I see, is the moon and a lot of stars. I starts to wonder about that and after a while I get tired and looks for a place to sit down. I am looking around, but is not able to find a nice place rest, so I just grab, some of these old books, that no one is reading anymore, most of them are black. After some minutes I am able to make me a nice place to sit, by putting several books together making them into a bench, and looking into the sky and wondering where the book came from, maybe that was a sign, that I am going to write a book of my own words, just following the signs. I pick up one of the old books and starts to to read, but is it so boring, no fun, that I start to make my own book, following my own destiny. Walking in the signs, is about to take shape.

The word is always written
Maybe it is some fiction
This is going to be action
Even at least some fraction

Poetry code book, 0.000336224112

misunderstanding
selves
want
souls
nice
humans
use
universe
love
wearing
soul
Within
True
earth
true
Without
world
share
show
like
goals
great
truth
Like
fear

Dove received a powerful light in his head, and woke up to life again. He feel lighter and like that he somehow had free open way to the universe, living with the world and not in the world. Like that there was something that he could not see and really explain, is was more like energy in the air, that surrounded him. In kind of way he feel light, but his body was just like the same.

He minded his dream, just before he waked up, he had a bad dream, about bullfighting. In his previous life he had passionate liked bullfighting, strong brave men that teared the bull, made it mad and tried to control the huge massive animal, with strong muscles. The long picture flashing dream was about that he was the ox itself. He was still lying in the bed wondering about his life. His past life, he wanted to have a better life this time. He got out of the bed, that was filled with the smell of the sweat of his body. He felt warm when he waked up, but now he is freezing. He got his clothes that was lying on a chair, beside the bed. He had a white loose fitted shirt and some gray trousers, feeling him free. The room was dark, telling him that it was still night. He looked at the watch on the night table, that told him that there was just some hours, that it was going to be the rise of the sun, that is going to turn from red to yellow, and rise high in the sky, the blue sky. While he got dressed, he though more and more about the dream, the dream was almost living. He was running into the stadium, and he looked at the man standing in the middle, with a big red cloth, long as his arm, that made him angry in some way, dark red is anger, maybe it was like that he was angry of being locked up in walls that surrounded his bull body. He wanted to smash into the red cloth, it felt like a firm wall, that he was going to punch, with his head, carried by the strong massive neck muscles and the deadly gore horns, because he had no arms that could putt away the red cloth, that was the only color that he could see in the gray view. He was so angry, he was so angry that he could not hear and see the crowd of people that was sitting on the tribunes of the stadium. He realized that this was a sign, from his soul or something, that the bull really have feelings. Feelings that is hurt able, that made him mad, to cover the feelings.

Earth is perfect
We are not
Emotions are good
Feeling are in harmony
Earth is a perfect world

He walked to the door, opened it and went out to the hall. He picked up a small bag and went into the living room, to get something to write on, a book with empty pages and lines waiting to be filled with a story, with maybe many words. He continued walking to the front door and opened the door carefully, to see that at the sky if this day was going to be sunny to. He smelled the fresh air, making him remember that this day was in the spring. The air was fresher, than the cold winter, and sharper than the hot and clammy summer, and more living, than the autumn, that smells like dead leaves. The sky was blue and he was going to out to feel the nature, maybe go for a trip to some mountain, and sit down and make some thoughts about what he was going to do in his new life, his second life.

Life is an exciting travel
That we not will cancel
Looking forward every day
The stars lead the way
Maybe as the angels pray

He is living in large city Zürich, of of the best living cities in the world, maybe it is helped by the sign of the city, where there are two lions caring about a castle, has help the city to become what it is. He lives not far from the rail way station in this world city, in the wonderful natural Switzerland. Lucerne is a nice city not a far from this city, so he is making a day to that city and its surrounding mountains. That will give him a nice feeling and free up all his thoughts in his mind. Male them into order.

He walked into the spring morning air, and felt like new, like the new fresh air of the spring, he was going to enjoy this day. Until the bad dream was out of his mind. After a couple of minutes he reached the rail station, while the sky was turning into morning red, the light red, the smiling red, the new day red. He bought a ticket and walked towards the train, the are s lot of people in the train station, some of the seems to be going to work, they are dressed up with business clothes, and having rush and sleep in their eyes, the are also some people that seems to be, like him making a trip, maybe to some friends and family. His friend of the day was going to be that nature, the growing nature, that feels refreshing, maybe write about it, so he can share his feelings with the people that do everyday work, people that makes this world staying together, making it like a society. They are his heroes, his true heroes.

He looks at the ticket and reads the seat number, and steps into the train. The seats are placed towards each other and separated with a small table. He is happy to have a seat with his face in the same direction of looking forward. He likes it that way, just like going into the future. People are different, in some cultures, they almost fight about having their backs towards the direction, maybe they feel it safer, and he is shore about to ask that question one day. He puts his bag at the next seat, and walks back out to get a cigarette. He lights the cigarette and looks at it and thinks that he should stop, it tastes empty, but the addict keeps him going on and on. It is strange that he feels the need of poison to stay alive. It is like that a firefighter is bringing wood to a fire, they are trying to put out. Maybe later is in his thoughts, and he realized that he is not completely new. He fills his body with the nicotine and steps back in the train. The wagon is filled with more people. Across of him there is a young lady, she is reading a book, she looks at him and he says, with a soft voice, trying to be polite and points at the seat, where he is going to sit.

«This is my chair, for the trip, and is making a small kind smile

«Take your site, she replies back, with a smile

«Thanks, he tells back, and moves his body toward his chair. He feels bad the smell of tobacco smoke in his cloths.

She sees that he feels bad, and that he is smelling his own body, and she takes her hand into the pocket and pulls out a light red candy, and asks, kindly with a carefully voice.

«Do you want one ?

«Thanks, he says and takes the candy and looks at her with a smile, little bit shy.

The train rolls quite and gently out of the station and the young lady dives into her book again, with magical words. Her eyes are walking the lines of words, in the book, and she looks like that the book and her body is one unit.

He feels better, just shortly after, and is looking around in the coupe, there are sitting two people across the middle walkway of the train. There is a lady and a man. The lady looks like a photo model, almost like some flashing memories of some photos of Marylin Monroe, opposite there is a man sitting with a camera, a large camera, seems to be good one. He picks up the notebook from his bag, and writes "train of fame, is the game" and continues with several words.

The young lady across him looks up from her book.. Without saying anything, just wondering, in silence. He recognize that she has moved out of the book world, and is looking at him, with an expression of what are you writing. He looks up from his book and at her kindly face and feels that he has to say something.

«I am a writer, a book writer

«Writing about what, she asks interested

«I don't know yet, just making some notes, maybe I will come up with something, the start and the end of books is aways difficult

«How ?

«Well, in the start, you have to make a good first impression, to keep the read wanting to continue, and the end has to be good so the read wants to read more books

She nods understanding and asks «Your first ?

«No, he answers with a tone, and cutting of the word making it sound like, I am not going to tell anymore.

«What is you name, she asks

«I write under a different name, but my name is Dove

«Why ? She asks

«Fame is hard though game, sometimes almost a deadly game, to write under a different name you can escape if you want

«I understand, she says and looks serious with a understandable expression in the lovely face

She dives into her magical words, that is written in the book again, and understands that he is kind of working, working with putting his words, and thoughts in his head down to the paper. There seems to be a lack of words from his mind. He looks up, and at the young lady. She recognize his looking and looks up. He feels a little bit bad about that he has disturbed her, and he thinks, and says

«Well, I am going to write this new book, and wonder what do you like to read ?

«Different subjects, but books that tells me something, and makes me think and wonder, maybe learn, maybe some romance, she smiles shy, with a romantic look in her eyes, that makes them shine. He waits a couple of seconds, until she has ready for a new question.

«What about nature ? He asks carefully

«That is nice, she says with a smile

«How ? He asks with a questioning face.

«Makes me living in the story, of the book, telling where I am

«Thanks, you are very kind, may I write it down and use it when I write my book ?

«Yes, she says with a proud voice

He picks up his note book and writes some words and sentences, with his pen. He stops and does some thinking. He looks at her and reorganize that she has not started to read again and asks her.

«I was also thinking about writing some culture, maybe what artist is thinking, trying to analyze what they where thinking.

«That is great, she says with a honest smiling voice

«Thanks, a lot, I have to write it down before I forget it. He dives into his book again, and writes a lot of words, some of them are sentences and some are headwords. He also make some sketching.

He starts to look out of the window, following with his eyes the passing still mirror looking lakes and the green fresh farming fields, brown cows, hunting the fresh grass between, yellow and white flowers. The fields are separated by stone fences. The pictures that he catches to his memory, gives him a pleasant feeling. Far away in the distance, he can see some of the mountains that is the the beginning of the alps. The alps that still is covered with show at the top of the mountains. In the mirror of the window he looks at her, she is very beautiful, having hair down to her shoulders, and there is something about her ,that makes him calm a pleasant feeling, just a warm soul feeling. He looks at her for long time, and tries to understand, why he is looking at her, there are something about her, but he can't put the words on the feeling, maybe good aura is the right word. He get a smell of her, it is like a lily or maybe like a alp flower Edelweiss.

He gets dizzy and lay his head back, into soft the chair and closes his eyes, and is ready of taking a look into the world of sleep. He gets a flashing pictures of staying in a old train, one of the trains that was made of wood, iron, dark black iron, covered with the particles of smoke of the coal, that was put into the heating kettle of the locomotive. The locomotive that pulls the wagons with its goods, and old fashion way of transportation. He opens his eyes and is happy about to be in a modern world, fast traveling world even if its covered of smells of modern interior, like synthetic fiber and air condition transporting away the smells, that is in the coupe. He closes his eyes again and falls shortly into sleep, a deep sleep without any dreams.

The train is slowing down its speed, fighting against the nature rules of gravity, until it is stopping and entering a train station, some people are leaving and some are entering the wagon. This is not his stop, so he is relaxed and watching the people. A woman is coming up to his seat, and shows him the ticket and takes place next seat to him. She is in the middle age, just like him, and she looks that she is going to work. Having neat style clothes, and a strong heavy perfume, matching to her strong karma. The train moves again, and she is picking up a computer from her bag, a black bag, with an design thats fits a woman, more like a large handbag. She starts the computer and is opening some documents, she reads and do some corrections of the text. Dove is looking and reading some of the documents, with moving his eyes, in that direction. He has to move his head some, and she recognized it. And he feels that he has to say something.

«I am a writer, a book writer

She looks at him, and stops for some seconds before she is saying, with a kind voice, after that she reads him, and understands that he is talk the truth.

«I am an advisor, in astrology and I am working on something about numerology. As you maybe have already read, she laughs carefully.

He laughs to, together with her, a kind laugh, not to load

«My eyes are not that good, but your subject is interesting, I know something about astrology, but numerology is a new word to me. Can you give me a short introduction ? He asks with a interesting kind attitude.

light
verse
Warming
Making
Love

«Thanks, talking is nice, writing is loneliness environment too.

«So you writing is your main job

«I have written some books and kind of live of the payment, but still want to say something to the readers, if they want. Anyway writing gives me pleasure and that is the most important thing to me.

«That is nice, sharing words in books is a nice thing, is my opinion.

«Thanks, he says with a proud voice, but not to proud, writers are often little bit shy.

«I have written a book to, but that was more like an academic book about my topic, astrology.

«Nice, but tell me about numerology, he asks interested

«It is not science

«That is not important to me, I just want to hear your opinion and make my own beliefs.

«That is true, very true. Good point, that is my opinion too.

«Tell me about the numerology, he says with a laugh, train is rolling

She gets the point, that he is very interested in the topic so she, turns her computer and show the screen so that he is able to read and look at the screen. She clicks at some programs shows a definition of the term. He reads the lines

Numerology *is any of many systems, traditions or beliefs in a mystical or esoteric relationship between numbers and physical objects or living things.*

Numerology and numerological divination were popular among early mathematicians, such as Pythagoras, but are no longer considered part of mathematics and are regarded as pseudo mathematics by modern scientists._This is similar to the historical relationships between astrology and astronomy, and between alchemy and chemistry.

Today, numerology is often associated with the occult, alongside astrology and similar divination arts.

The term can also be used for those who, in the view of some observers, place excess faith in numerical patterns, even if those people don't practice traditional numerology.

Modern numerology often contains aspects of a variety of ancient cultures and teachers, including Babylonia, Pythagoras, *astrological philosophy from Hellenistic* Alexandria, *early* Christian mysticism, *the occultism of the early* Gnostic's, *the* Hebrew *system of the* Kabbalah, *The Indian* Vedas, *the Chinese* "Circle of the Dead", *and the* Egyptian.

«So if this is occult, can it be used in a good manner ? I am in a way, given a second chance in my life, like got a new life. He says quite.

«Interesting, yes you can use it to find your self, together with many many many others aspects, like astrology, inheritance, living environment, how you look, how you treat your self. Humans are complicated, our brains make us super animals, she laughs.

«I understand, but I don't quite understand, but do you have an example. He says with a smile

«Thanks of asking, she says and turns the computer back in front of her, so that she is able to handle it easier. She performs many click and turns the computer back to him, so that he is able to see the screen again.

«Do you know the American presidents, that one who is now and the last one ?

DNA

Is what the science say

Counted in the soul DNA

In our blood it flows

Pairs in colorful rows

It can be counted in astro colors
Like what our eyes follows
It can be counted in numbers
Until everybody stop wonders

«Yes, he answers, after a short thinking break, and recalling them with pictures of how they look in his mind.

«They are public, so I use them as examples. The one before, George Bush, had 15/6, 15/6, 16/7 and 17/8, the existing one, Barak Hussein Obama Jr has 20/2, 17/8 , 18/9 and 17/8.

«These are just some numbers, what do they say

«Some say that larger number are the better, but there are some many factors, these examples are counted out of birth and the name. Do you know Dalai Lama ?

«Yes, that bold one with the wearing monk's habit that are red and some yellow

«He is not born with his name, but as young he was given his name, and has these numbers 22/4, 33/6, 17/4 and 11/2. As young they where taking care of him and given training. Buddhist believe in reincarnation, so when one Dalai Lama dies, they tries to find one that is born, after and closes up to his death. 33/6 is a master number. There is some references to astrology, I am working on that part.

«How is that connected ?

«In western astrology, we have something called cardinal cross. We divide often astrology into circles. To illustrate it it is like a tube, a transparent tube, showing the DNA inside and covered with the personal numbers in one part of the tube and the astrology connection in the other side of the tube, and there is links, synchronism links between them, making a connection, showing who you are. If you want to use it or not it is up to you.

She click at an presentation at the computer and show the following screen.

Ascendant or rising sun tells about the outer of you, a simplified expression of what one is in possession of, the first impression others get. The descendant is the point directly opposite, or 180 degrees away from the ascendant and refers to partners or relationships.

Midheaven: How our public, professional face to the world. Often role (chair, student, dentist, plumber etc) and how one expresses the professional role they have. The Imum Coeli is said to refer to our roots and also to the least conscious part of ourselves. It symbolizes foundations, beginnings in life, what may have been experienced through parental inheritance and homeland influences, need for security and relationships with the home and family life.

«That was a lot of teaching, rocket science to my head. I really have to think about it, may I take some notes, so I can read about it later ?

«Yes you may, this is complicated, just an introduction of the topic. She says with a smile and a laugh, and continues with «It is also mathematic and psychological. A strange combination, but also some truth, if used correctly, use the best parts and use is in a positive manner.

He turn back to his note book and starts to write, to looks at the computer screen and carries on with that until he is finished. Then he returns to her and says

«I still don't see how it can be used, but I will maybe think about it. This was to much information to me, so I have to relax, maybe get some sleep, before I can continue on my trip. He says with a tied voice.

She smiles and nods in an understandable mode and says. «It is like going to an psychological session. You feel like empty, but the main thing, you remember the essence of the words, and if you need them later in your life, you can use it to self personality treatment.

He nods, and puts his notebook back at his bag and turns firmly back to his softs seat to get some rest. He closes his eyes and heads for dream land.

The young woman has been listening, and is looking like a questioning mark, She looks like that she wanted to read and look at what they was talking about. She didn't ask, and didn't wanted to disturb them.

He reorganize that she is following their conversation and looks at her and asks

«Sorry about that I didn't ask what you are doing, I was completely in my own mind and my thoughts.

She smiles and is happy about that he is asking, her questions had really hit his mind and says

«That is fine, I am a student

«Great, he says with a smile and continues with the following question

«What are you studying ?

«I am thinking about, working with society, sociology, I do not know yet what I am going to be yet. That education gives me a lot of possibilities

«That seems to be a nice, choice, many possibilities, when I was at your age, there was not so many possibilities

«Writing books is interesting, covering many different subjects, she says with a voice, that makes him proud

«That is right, but writing books is a kind of lonely task in this modern society.

«It is never to late to change, she says

«You are right about that, but now I have started my journey and going to write a book, it is like putting a task to myself. Maybe I will make some plans during the book writing and follow your advise. Thanks a lot, you are maybe born to with something about society

She smiles and nods

The woman, that is working with astrology says to them both

«This is a good example of how we can use astrology in the future, as a part of an advisor in life. In the early live, giving help of choosing what to be, and how to get an education, that is fitted to that. Maybe make an wide education, like you and possibilities are many.

«Walking into an idealistic world, everyone , he says

She looks at him, and really do some thinking, and says to him

«You are a bright man

«Thanks, he says with a proud voice, and continues with. I need some sleep, had some bad dreams this night and have a long journey in front of me.

They are all stopping talking and getting back to their chairs of doing what they started to do. He look out of the window for some minutes and the green fields make him sleepy.

Talking is when we share
To every lovely dear
Our feelings about true love
That humans show
In truth in aesthetics way
Like poetry we say

Time is how we use our lives to live
Being caring positive
In true love to other humans
Without any burdens
And in harmony with the earth
Pleasuring every child birth

He wakes up just some minutes before the train arrived Lucerne. He has sleep in his eyes, and the view feels foggy, the body feels a little bit out of place, but shortly he is coming more and more into the real world. The young woman is gone, he thinks that maybe that she has got out of the train at a earlier stop. The model and the photographer across the midway of the train is looking out of the window. He wonders if they are looking at the countryside to. Several houses with the alp look, dark brown roofs, wide dark brown roofs, in a kind of way, making them looking quite different of the houses that the rest of the world, and that makes him happy, it is the memorable image of the soul of the houses, in this amazing beautiful green country with frosted mountains, separated by rushing rivers, that lead the water from the snow into the deep cold lakes.

The train arrives the station, built in a modern way, lots of clear glass with leading the light of the sky into the halls, that protects the travelers from from any weather, burning sun to chilly rain, summer heat to winter freezing cold. He steps out of the train, happy to be at the move, feeling that his body is coming back to how he was born, a human body, that is able to walk and grab, and having a logical brain that is useful of doing rational things.

He walks towards the old wooden bridge of the city. The Chapel bridge, the landmark of the city, that was built to protect the city. The wooden bridge gives him a felling of stepping back in time, while looking at the painted pictures that is covered inside, the bridge that has red roofing tiles, and watertight wooden fence, reaching up to his stomach. He walks almost to the middle of the bridge, and stops to enjoy the view of the lake, that has the pictures of the frosty mountains, in the water, as a mirror. There is an old castle, up at a clip to the right of the middle of the lake, is is quite far away, and he remembers that he was up at that castle at a dinner with some friends in his past life. They drove up the road, that was climbing like a snake , and passed the head, and went into a open free space, where the castle was. They enjoyed a nice dinner with red wine, and was looking back at the city, that was lightened up of the city lights, different colors of red, yellow and white lights, making the city almost magical in the dark night. While enjoying the amazing view, he is wondering about walking up to one of the other monuments, of the city, the dying lion, that was made as a memorable stone statue of falling swiss guards. He wonder about it, for some time, and agrees with himself, that the memory of the words told by the writer Mark Twain “the most mournful and moving piece of stone in the world.“ gives him enough words in his mind, to picture the lion, telling the mood and aesthetic view.

He is looking at the mountains and is getting the feeling that he wants to be at the top of the largest mountain, Mount Blanc, that is created by the nature, as Europe largest monument, separating Europe into two parts north and south. That is a place where he can clear his thoughts and wondering about what he is going to do in rest of his life. There was a reason why he waked up again, so he makes a plan in his head how to get there.

He walks to the end of the bridge, and there are the Marilyn Monroe copy and the photographer working together, They are making pictures of her and the view of the lake as the background. He stops and is looking at them and watches how the photographer works, and he walks up behind him, and looks how the photographer is thinking. The photographer reorganize that he is watching them and turns around and says.

«Do you take photos too. I heard at the train that you are a writer. Sorry about that, but I got long ears, he laughs

«No, I don't make photos, but I do some drawing

«Have you tried, if you are able to draw, you got knowledge about aesthetics.

«Maybe, you are right about that, maybe I will try later, good advice, he says with a smile

«By the way, my long ears heard that you where talking about DNA

«Yes, that is right, he says with a laugh. Laughing to the comment about the long ears.

«I just have to tell you, I wanted to tell you at the train, but I didn't want to be rude, but I watched a program at TV, and that was about that we men, have a Y chromosome, and that goes in inheritance

«Maybe that is right, but I don't see how that is connecting to our conversation at the train. Except the word DNA, he says with a large smile

«It was just that hit my mind, if you are going to write about it, you can put on that we seems to all descend from some clever people in Africa, it is mentioned in the bible as Adam. The meaning of the name Adam, is human, so strong and clever men seems to have a connection down to maybe fifty thousands years.

«Still don't see the connection

«You are a clever man, they told you, so you got a strong DNA inheritance and together with the astrology and the numerology, you can find out what you are best at doing.

«Good though. I will write it on my mind, he laughs

«You are welcome, I have to work, my product is getting bored and loosing her focus, at her job.

«So she is the product and you are the producer, but I am very very proud of her, she is my girl friend too. She is my hero, and he laughs

«Yes, and she is going to be famous, producers are not. She is the product, the brand. He laughs and turns back to his work.

He walks to a shop nearby and get some clothes, that keeps him warm of the trip up the mountain. He looks at quality of the clothes and not the brand, quality is more important, than the brand of his trip, there can be windy and freezing cold at the top. He also gets him self a snowboard, it is easier to carry and is making him flowing lighter in the snow and, the main reason is that he can have some fun racing down the hill in speed, than walk down the hill in the return. In somehow, he looks at the colors, the clothes and the board. he wants them to match, he wants some style, even if his trip is going to be alone, but maybe it gives him a nice feeling, feeling complete. He walks happy out to the lake and is looking for for some transport, a boat that cuts the mirror water into two half's, while making enjoyable speed, speed that takes him fast away, to the other side where he can start his trip up to the mountain. There are several boats, mostly large boats, walks around and finally finds a white speed boat, the shines in the light of the sun, and in the light of the water, making it glitter like shining stars that covers the black sky in the nights. He walks up the driver and asks

«Are you vacant ?

«Yes I am, the driver answers, with a firm steady voice, making him comfortable to take the drive with him

«I am going across the lake, I am going to the top of the largest mountain

«Just jump aboard, he answers

Dove gets into the speed boat, with his baggage, and a enthusiastic mind. The boat driver places his things underneath the deck and makes a sign to him to take place in the other chair, that is close up the front window of the boat.. Dove reaches out his hand towards the drivers hand, shakes it and is says

«I am Dove, he says with a smile

«Nice to meet you, he says without telling his name, and continues with saying, take place, this is going to be a windy trip.

«Nice to hear, he says and places himself firm in the chair, that is covered with light brown bail.

The driver unties the ropes, that was holding the boat, and makes it moving fast forward, with a left turn out from the dark wooden quay, and leaving white topped waves, too both sides, making it looking like an arrow traveling across the lake. Dove is looking at the nature, the are light green, fresh leaves, at the threes down to the lake, while he is enjoying the speed of the boat, making him feel alive. The trip takes a while, and he enjoys every minute of the trip, and knows that he will remember it, maybe a memory of life. The boat slows down when it reaches the other side of the lake, and the driver places the boat up to a dark wooden quay, that has a road covered with small shingle up to a house, that has a signboard telling that it is a hotel. He gets his things and tells the driver, thanks of the trip in a happy mode, and walks up the the hotel. When he enters inside door, he is meet with a smell of food, nice aromatic smelling food, food smell that makes him hungry. He decides to take a break before he continues the trip, to the white mountain, with the helicopter, that he has ordered, with help of the staff at the hotel. While waiting of his transportation, he makes a long tasteful lunch in the enjoyable balcony with a view of the lake and it surroundings, with the lake, wood above it, the castle and a mountain. A large mountain called Mount Pilatus.

Below the balcony, there are some sheep's, white ones, that is eating the green grass that grows, on the spring fields, that covers everywhere. They are in in their own world, hunting of the grass of food. He walk up to them and watch them, wonder how they think, are they happy to in their share of their part of their world, be feeders to the rest of the world. He feels that they are telling him something, just like that they are telling him, to be like the others, staying in their orders. He doesn't understand their words, he wants to write the words with his own sword, that is his new world, that is what he is told.

Later in the day, his transportation is arriving, and it is a white helicopter, and it is called the white eagle. The helicopter is landing in front of the hotel, and the sheep's are afraid and run away. The large engine bird is disturbing their world of peace, even if they do not have emotions in their faces, but their eyes are able to show fear.

He enters the white wonder machine, with his snowboard and his bag, and is his way to the white mountain, the large white frosty mountain. They travel fast and passed woods, green fresh spring woods in the hillsides, mirror lakes far beyond them, and riding along with mountains, like a roller coaster. They follow the valleys in their trip to the white frosty mountain. The trip is a long trip and he is enjoying the nature, with is wonderful feature, it is like music in his head, when he follows contours of the mountains, making dramatic tones, making a symphony. He picks up his note book and makes some sketches of the nature and figures how he can put words to these mountains.

The helicopter is reaching the white mountain, and the pilot tells him, that it is to windy to take him to the top, and he agrees about that since the top of the mountain is showing the blowing show, traveling like snow crystals, like making a jet stream in a horizontal line of the top of the white mountain, lightened by the sun, and having the blue sky behind, the top of the mountain, that looks like an pyramid. The driver takes the helicopter to a plateau in front of the top, and he jumps out of the helicopter into the soft snow that feels like white cold cotton. He waves back to the helicopter, making a sign of that he is happy and thankful of the trip, his on time trip, to this mountain. He fights him threw the light snow, that flows with the wind he moves his body, to the edge of the plateau, where it is easier to walk the rest part of his trip. At the edge, there is an proud large ibex, that looks like an Capricorn, looking at him, it is looking at him with steady firm eyes at him, watching where he is going to move. He feels is and is it like telling him, this is my world, this is where I live, you may visit me, but you can't stay here forever, you are human and your body is not build to life in these freezing show crystals that flows in the wind, day and night, even in summer. He understands that the animal is telling the tones of the mountains, and it is like poetry, tones of the mountains, just like poetry of the human DNA, the poetry of the mountains is the DNA of nature, that he is fighting. While he understands this, he understands, that he has to walk to the top of the mountain, to understand what direction his soul and his body and his mind is going to take in the nearby feature. He find this magical creature fascinating and the wind blows threw the horns and makes a sound like trumpets, making him remember the sound of trumpets in the pictures of many visions of angels blowing their trumpets telling that life is music, emotions are music, waves blowing in the DNA making different music and emotions to the soul. Different DNA's have different music, telling their lives. Stories to be told in music, poetry and emotions, good emotions. He walks towards the top and feels every snow crystals and he starts to wonder about that there are not a single snow crystal that is comparable, everyone is different, some of them are fitting together and some of them are not. The landscape up to the top of the mountain is covered with several crystals, that makes a carpet beyond his feet, a think soft carpet that carries him to the top, making him able to walk to to top and listen to the wind, where his life is going to start. He fights him self threw the wind, and he does not give up even if the wind makes him freezing and making his cheeks freezing red, almost telling him that this walk should he stop. He carries his way to the top and he gives him a feeling like a king making his way to the top. He stops at the top and starts listening to the winds. They blow from all angels and his intuition tells him to follow the warm wind, coming from the ocean in the Mediterranean sea and the desert that stays on the other side of the ocean, a different continent. He listen for a long time to the wind, and follows his sign and put his snowboard at his feet's and is heading down for a cottage to start to write his next book, the book of signs, telling what the universe is telling him, with the help of the angels and what signs they show in everyday life and how everything is putting together to make this earth into a complete society, a living planet with the protection of the ozone layer, from the strong radiation sun rays, that would killed everything on this planet. He understands that the earth cannot exist without clean water and the heating sun.

Peace, please

Melody: Knockin' on heaven's door, Bob Dylan

Peace, please, Peace, please

Just look at the sun, in the blue blue sky
We don't have to lie, we are all very very shy
I don't wonder why, Angels can fly
In the blue blue sky, we all can even try

We just have to believe in angels now
We just have to believe in angels now
We just have to believe in angels now
We just have to believe in angels now

Earth we do not have to burn, we all have to learn
We can share, just to everywhere
Close your eyes, look at the sun
Heaven is what we see, just trust what you feel

Peace, just please, Peace, just please
Peace, just please, Peace, just please
Peace, just please, Peace, just please
Peace, just please, Peace, just please

Peace, please, Peace, please
Peace, please, Peace, please

start
just
hero
flowing
Change
moon
falling
Power
chart
Walking
loving
magical
energies
love
hear
shown
glowing
wonder
gone
every
feel
wonderfull
new
Magical
wonderful
going
magic
forever
everywhere
heart
angel

The wonderful couple, Maria and Carl is in the bedroom, it is nice and dark, some light of other buildings are heading through the curtains. The walls are white, but the dark night makes them not able to see the walls, but some pictures can be seen, of the tiny light that is heading threw the curtains, from the light from the city, colorful pictures with figures reminding of the the thoughts of some great painters in the past. The floor is covered with soft wall-to-wall curtain, making it soft and pleasant to get out of the bed. The bed is a great king size bed, in the colors of white and light gray.

Carl suddenly wakes up middle of the night and turns around and shakes Maria, carefully.

«Wake up woman. He says it with a calm voice. He waits for some seconds and tell her again with a higher voice and a hand, that shakes her gently again, with more power in his movements.

«Wake up woman

«Stop calling me that! She says, with a load voice, she had wakened the first time.

Carl stops for some seconds and tells her, with a pleasant voice, so that she is in a mood of listening to what he is going to say. He is trying to say it in a lovely tone, without overplaying his way of telling.

«Wake up, sweetie!

«Why are you waking me up middle of the night. I have an important day at work tomorrow.

«I got a call!

«I can't hear anything, go to sleep, dear

«I really got a call!!

«I don't understand what you are saying, she says

«I got a call, really!!!

«From whom, may I ask, my dear.

«From God

«From God ? Hahahaha

«You are very funny sometimes, but now it is middle of the night.

«But I did!!!!

«Did he fall down from his cloud and into this room ? Into our apartment in the golden city.

«He waked me into a dream.

«That must be "dream come true", as you always say.

«Something like that! Yes!

«Since you already have wakened me and make me smile, middle of the night, I want to hear your fairy tail, maybe you got to much beer with the "gentlemen" at the baseball match.

«Don't complain about my friends. We are having fun time, we really have some interesting discussions, one of the guys are going to calculate how to make the perfect throw one day, but you are a woman, so how an you understand our enjoyment. But yesterday, I didn't drink too much. I am going to meeting tomorrow, with my boss, maybe he has good news.

«So he is your God ?, the great great God in your life, and told you something in your dreams and makes you awake middle of the night. This dream is going to make a perfect meeting, with your God.

«Why are women always talking so much ? I have something to say, and this is the most important thing in my life.

«Your boss?

«Stop!Stop!Stop! Please listen. Can you do that for me?

«Yes, when you give me that wonderful smile , you are really nice and you are the true you!

«You remind me of my favorite teddy bear, when I was a kid. That is why I love you. This tells me that you have a sweet heart underneath your silly masks, that you where at work and with your friends. Well what are you going to tell me? Don't be shy, great great husband. You are my God, Did you know that.

«This is really serious, so stay sharp.

«God told me: Jesus is going to Mekka!

«Hahahahahaha, what did you say ?

«Jesus is going to Mekka!!

«Hahahahahaha

«Jesus is going to Mekka!!!

«You have always been a funny man. I love you, please hold me and give me a kiss, a kiss, so that we can sleep and be ready for a new exiting and beautiful day.

«It is not an joke!!!!!!!!!!!!!

«Don't get angry, you know that, I don't believe in your God faith and you have never asked really about my faith. We just are different. You live on Mars and I live on Venus.

«Here she goes again, talking, talking, talking, talking...

«I have to do this, this is going to be my biggest business opportunity in my life. Since God told me this, too only me, just me, the great great me, the boss, I am going to makes us rich, rich, rich. I am getting out of bed and start working.

«You seems to be serious, but I don't understand you. Why do you wants to be rich ?

«I am going to buy that building to you my dear. That building! With fifty levels of black shining glass, reflecting the soul of God, as he waves gently like the king, from his cloud.

«And when you have done that ?

«I am going to be richer and richer, buying the whole city, to you my dear.

«And so after that ?

«Damn, I can't plan my whole life, lifetime is long time, if you are able to count to ten, or maybe you are just able to think silly colors of your paintings and the gallery you are running, making people think that art is living. Give me a dollar bill and then I am going to show you a picture of real art. Money talks, money walks. The art of living.

«I am so sorry my my dear, but I am making the real money in this house

«What! Are telling me a fairy tail again?

«Whatever! You are the sweetest man in the world. I really hope that you are able to buy me some flowers one day. By the way it is your life, and I have to sleep. Sleep at the sofa, my funny dear.

«Good night, see you tomorrow!

«Sometimes I wonder why God told me to marry you!

What did you say, this is getting really really interesting.

«I said, I am getting my blanket and my pillow, and running to my working room, with my desk and my nice nice soft sofa. Made of steel and 1 inch of red soft cotton. Maybe my back, so it is going to have a better look tomorrow than ever, so you love me more than you ever have done.

«Do you really remember how we got together ?

«Yes, I really do in fact, I am the clever guy, making the impossible, possible.

«I think you have to tell me that story once again. None of us can sleep anyway, «Clack. Remember to take on your superman costume next time you fly out of the window, maybe your stomach won't make the fall to hard this time.

«This is enough. Let us be kids, make a pillow war and then suddenly get back in collage and make love again, like we did. «We where like the stock marked, up and down. We where like rabbits.

«That was then, maybe I liked it. Women like sex too, men don't have patent on sex.

You are the most sensitive beer can, in the world, Your highness, with direct line to God, The chosen one, the great human one, are you done? Tell me more, and that is for shore!

«You where so lucky, that I let you have me as your boyfriend, and later on your faithfully husband, letting my strong hands be your protector of your human angel body, that shines all day long.

«Your strong hands is a result of your work out with all the beer cans, my lovely husband. I don't know how you can be unfaithful, so tell me more!

«All the girls was trying to get me. Every day, when I came to to school in the coolest car, girls looked at me and told me with their eyes. Swinging their bodies, to make them even more sexy, than they already where. I wanted them all, but you was the sexiest girl. At the whole school, in the whole city, in the whole country, in whole the world, in the whole universe.

«You told me then, you have so niiice hair, it looks like angel hair. I can imagine that your hair blows softly when, When I get you in my topless car, and we drive far far into the highway, with lightning speed, this is going to be my way, far far away or no way.

«A man got to do his best when he is going to get the best angel in the world

«What did you think really about my personality, was I a human or just a nice looking sculpture, that you wanted to be in your collection

«The first move had to be right, I needed to do something special, to get you home into my heart

«That worked very well, and then you told me your beautiful, poem you have written, and I think it is the only poem that you ever have written.» It went like this

Just do it!

We are the best

Fuck the rest

We did it!

Yeahhhhh! Signed with your personal signature. Your lover boy forever, and the note, kiss me hard, I am not an retard.

«Now you are making me in horrible position's. I don't know what to say or if I am going to say. I want to play in the fairway, if that is ooookeyyyyy!

«Lets get dressed and move to the kitchen I am getting thirsty of all your talking.

«Sometimes you can be clever, I need a beer or maybe ten.

«You are my gentleman, with style. The smoking is in the closet, if you know how to open it?

«very funny, haha, princess Leia, I am with the force, remember?

«Sometimes you are funny, just coming out of the cave, if you are able to spell that word. C A V E

«Damn Lana, I can't find a clean T-shirt

«Maybe some of them forgot to walk out of the washing machine, if you know what that is, the ghost machine in that scary room, that you hate of all your heart.

«That is spooky, I am scared, mummy, help me, help me, that monster is going to eat me

She walks hasty away and returns with some clean T-shirts, throwing them into his hands

«Nice my love, my dear dear love, the boss is always the boss, never wrong, because HE is the boss.

«Let us talk about that later

They are getting dressed, in a anger way, and are walking towards the door, the calm atmosphere, that lived in the room just past away, just like an hurricane went into the house and picked up the humans in the middle of the night.

Houses
lie
selves
shelves
friends
stay
careless
protect
times
spend
Staying
acting
family
happiness
Happy

How we meet

The kitchen is in a modern style. Oak look is the main color, and some steel and gray. She had used many hours to get this result, together with the drawer, maybe an art mind makes is nice, real teamwork is showing off. He dumps into one of the chairs and is looking at the lovely wife that he has got. She gets herself a glass of water and finds a beer to her husband

«Here you go, my sweetie

«Thanks

He looks into the table and says

«This call is very very important to me

«A call middle of the night is always important, we should be in bed to get ready for tomorrow. I am sorry that I was a bit grumpy

«A bit, it was like the dragon has wakened, the heat of the the flames, made me scared

«You know that I need the sleep. Sleep is important to me to get things done, in the real word. You need really to listen to me

«You are talking in codes sometimes, and I don't understand what you are saying.

«I am very happy to hear that you admit that. Living is hard out there, and we need to stick together, nobody seems to care anymore!

«Now you are starting talking in codes again. I will get us rich

«I am going to support your call, if you just tell me the true story about how we fell in love.

«I agree, truth, no more cross fingers and legs.

«It have been years since, I heard that story, that story is making me living and feeling, we get the harmony back in our lives, and we are one unit.

«Damn you are so soft, like cotton

«Maybe you could try it some day.

«That is impossible, I am the man, and the man don't have feelings outside the apartment. What are my buddies going to say, if I am tell them, damn he missed that ball. I am going to cry, please hold my beer and popcorn.

«Maybe the world needs more feeling in the public.

«The world is going to be crazy, if soldiers started to talk about feeling. I can't kill that man, it hurt my feelings

«Is that bad?

«Who is going protect us, then ?

«Protect?

«You really don't understand us men, we got the power, the force is with us

«Stop that movie talk, and tell me the story

«Yes, princess Leia, I will do, let the force be with us, my sister

«Grow up, my son

«Yeah, yeah, as you wish

The story started with that my family moved to this city. I had to change the school, and I had to make an big impression of the new school. My parents was rich, so clever me, talk to them, so I could get a new car, a car with style. They agreed about that. It was like that they said

«My son is the best, so we will give you the best. You are the heart in the chest.

«You don't know who you are, but I am waiting, continue the story, my dear

«I got really hot, my mom helped me with clothes, together with a expert, Mr. HowToGet popular, damn, I love my parents money

«Don't get off the track now

«Well I asked my buddies, who are she?

«She is impossible, she is acting like an angel, flying around, working very hard and always perfect.

«I didn't tell them that you was the prettiest angel I ever seen. You was like magic, I just could feel it.

«You are so sweet, when you talk from your heart.

«Don't make me soft, woman

«How old are you?

«Still growing, every day, I am going to be big, really big, the biggest man in the world.

«Continue with your story, that is a large step forward, on this earth

«It was impossible, to get near you, my talk just went of you, just like that you are bullet proof. I had to change, but how. I went to a pro, and told him about the situation. Still love my parents money, they where so great

«Continue!

«He asked my lot of questions, h made me discover that you where taking a class in drama. You where working so hard in all other classes, so there was no possibilities

«That is your door, he said

«Are you crazy? Me taking a drama class, no way, man.

«You act every day, he told me

«Every day?

«Yes, at school, you act to be the world best in sports, at your parents, you do it now. You play different roles all day long.

«You are kidding me, I need a real pro, you need to go to a real mind shrinker, I lost the match, I could not get you, but something always told me to never give up. I was really good in sports, girls was so....

«Hey, hey hey, stop that, please

«Before the last summer, my buddies and I went to a trip, we had a lot of beers, we was surfing and had a really great time. We really got drunk a lot of times, haha

«Oh, stop it, that is not so interesting.

«Well something was missing.

«Maybe you needed something

«Oh stop it, my father was making the money, just like my grand father. I am going to be a great man one day

«Yeah yeah, just keep up with the story

«I went back to that Pro, later on, and I told him that I could not take a course in acting. I have a reputation to my parents, my buddies, to the school, to the society, to the world, to the universe.

«In somehow he told me, go to this woman, she has special abilities, almost like magic.

«I went crazy, and told him just I don't trust them. I will do it my way and that is the right way, the highway.

He told me «give it a shoot! Nobody knows, just be an undercover agent, and get into her office. And by the way, why do you want her?

«Then I discovered, I have to say it, I smashed my hand into the table, and shouted "She is an angel"

He said «I know, I just had to make you tell me that. Go for it, just do it, go go go go!

«You talk just my coach

«Yes, I am you coach, your life coach

«I will give it a shoot. so I did. I sent her an e-mail, told her the story. I was just like writing a story in class. I did it. She asked me to come, to her, at her office. I just said, no way. She asked me to go for an drive. Well that seems to be nice, I am driving, but we are driving in places where nobody knows me. She told me

«That is fair.

We made an appointment, I picked her up, and she was nice, she talked to me, like some of these nice teachers, made me comfortable. I trusted her. After a couple of meetings, I agreed to get up in her office. I went into the office looked aground, and then I got froze to ice, just like an sculpture. At the wall there was the same poem, as the poem you read at school, at the performance. That one about the eyes, soul, hair and so one.

«Don't you remember it?

«I am telling you the story, not the poem

«Just a second

She runs away, and are coming back with a picture, there is was, the poem and tells him, with a smiling voice with great feeling

«Sorry, dear, but the poems belongs to the story

«Yeah, yeah, you are right

«You are a really nice man, continue

«Well I learn it, since my own poem didn't work

She smiles, with the feeling of the soul, she knows that he is able to write poems, but not letting the feeling, becoming a part of the poems.

«Why are you smiling that way ? I still don't understand

«Some secrets are to be hidden, it is just a woman thing, as you say.

«Well, that is really really true

«Do you remember it?

«No, I can't

«I understand, she smiles

«Continue, God is waiting

«What?

«Never mind

«Well I learn it then, almost

«Yes, almost

I was walking around, figuring how to do do it. Then I got the idea, my great great idea.

«You have never told my your great great idea

«Men got to have secrets too

«Yes, they do

«I am the genius, that is why he told me

«Please finish the story, my dear

«Well as you remember, we just crashed into each other. I took you hands and I told you, and looked into your eyes.

The beauty of a woman

The beauty of a woman,
isn't the clothes she wears
The figure that she carries,
or the way she combs her hair

The beauty of a woman,
must be seen from in her eyes,
Becomes that's the doorway to her heart,
the place where love resides.

The beauty of a woman,
isn't in a facial mole,
But true beauty in a woman,
is reflecting by her soul.

It's the caring that she cares to give,
the passion that she shows,
And the beauty of a woman,
With passing years only grows.

«Then you kissed me, and that was the story

«Remember, the truth, the story did not end there.

«Well, the truth, was

«Well?

«The truth was that I felt something special, when I hold your hands.

«I just got a strange imagine of that I connected to your soul, just like a yellow light, like magic

«Your run away, and I just got my hands in the air and shouted

«I BELEIVE IN GOD!

«People started to laugh, but I didn't care. I was kissed by an angel

«May I kiss you again, my dear.

«Lets go to bed, and make a good warm kiss, that really makes us feel

She smiles, it is like hear heart is gloving, and the whole body is shining

«You smiles so funny, what about your sleep, You was complaining

«Later, later my dear, lets go

«Maybe you are a man

«You bet, I am, code maker!

They walks back to the bed room, and a different wind is entering the room, just like a warm lovely wind with the power of magic, connecting souls together in true love, committed by souls.

Pleasure is when we use our souls

In true love to our souls

And in harmony to other humans

Day at work

Good morning sunshine
This day is wonderful fine
It is a new healthy shiny day
A nice beautiful warm day
The heart will lead the way

The day started pretty hasty and there had not been to much sleep, so they both rush to their jobs, to make meetings.

She went to her gallery and had an important meeting with a new artist. She was making completely new art. Pictures with messages and beauty that is excellent.

He went to his office, the newspaper of the finance world. He had his mind of the call and was going to tell that to his boss. He entered the meeting room. Black chairs and an big meeting room table was in the middle of the room. The light is quite good, which makes is comfortable and peaceful. He walk to the coffee machine, and makes a thought, we do we always have to drink coffee, why not a beer og maybe some Champaign, make some happy meetings. Well if this was was my company, I would have less rules, let people work, be happy, get the best out of every employee. Have some really fun time, smiling people, almost like moving like dancing, in happiness.

«God morning boss

«God morning, you seems to be in a good mood, what is up ?

«haha, my wife had some happy time last night

«Nice, really nice, love is the true life of living, that is what is making us heading forward into the future.

«Yes! That is true.

«Well I am going to make your day, into a bad day

«I am sorry to tell you that the owners of this magazine has told me to stop the whole business. The are just bad money these days

«Bad money?

«We are not selling enough magazines, with sad stories about companies that is going broke.

«Yes, I agree that, life is hard these days, maybe we need a new start.

«Well not in this company

«So what does that mean

«We are firing everybody in six months

«That is great!

«What?

«I was coming today to tell you that I have a new mission in life.

«What is that?

«I got a call

«From whom

«From HIM!

He points his finger towards the sky

«What, are you crazy

«Maybe or maybe not.

«Whatever, that is your life. Well the owners of this company has told me to make deals. The deal is that you will receive three months salary if you quit today or work six months to the bitter end

«That is great, deal, that is what I feel

«Damn, I am making you happy, and that makes me happy to. Live today, worry tomorrow.

«I am going for my call

«What did he tell you

«That is a secret

«You can tell me

«No, I can't, because this is a really really good news to the whole world.

«haha, Are you going to be Jesus ?

«No, my boss, I am just the writer

«Write how Jesus become bankrupted. Anyway. Good luck, and call me when you are finished with your work, there are still a lot of matches in the world series

«yes, we don't want to miss them, they are making our daily lives happy

«True happiness

«With a lot of beers and fantastic performance

«see you around

«Thanks a lot my former boss

«The secretary will make your the contract, women are nice to do work

«Yes, we think and they work

«Just the truth, we are the great ones.

«Bye

«Bye

He feels really happy, so he walks to buy some cookies, and shares them with the rest of the office. This company was really good, better that the stock marked.

He shakes hands with everybody and with a happy smile he is heading to the pub, to celebrate that he is fired, maybe God made it happened. In the pub, he was thinking about his new project, making small notes, how to make it. He didn't want to get drunk because he had a great work to do. So he went home, he needed Internet to start research, the world treasure of information, in the digital world. The world who connects people around the earth, even into the space.

The great finance story

He arrives, the apartment later, and is entering the hall.

«Hello, sweetie

«Hello, my love. Wow, you are really happy, give me a kiss

«Hey, you are not the boss

«What are you saying

«I will give you a kiss, when I feel to do it.

«You are the boss, I am very happy to see and hear that you follow your feelings

He walked to her and give her a nice kiss

«That is why I am supporting you in your great "Call"

«Thanks my angel, I feel very alive and I got fired today, but I got some money. Three months of payment.

«That is great, but I am worried about it. I do not want to have the trouble we got after your big investment at Wall Street

«That was just bad luck

«I think that was the problem, you just went, luck, not doing your homework really. By the way why did you get fired at work ?

«The owners didn't make any money on telling sad stories, companies that is going broke.

«Yes, that is for shore, I am happy that that work ended. It make you sad, it made us sad, but now you just changed back to the man I married, the man I love, the man I admire.

«You are really nice, my love. You make me strong. I am a really lucky man, God is go great, and he gave you, my angel, as a gift.

«You are strong, but I have to remember you of that project that nearly went wrong with you life.

«That project was so great, but it was just bad luck

«I remember last time you told me that, you got a call, that was that summer after collage, we was going to university at that music festival

«But that was really true

«Let me tell you what I think

«Come on, tell me

«You was so drunk and I think you had taken some acid too, can you admit that now

«Well

«Well, speak out

«Well I did, I can't lie anymore

«That is my true man

«Well but I got a call, or it was just like a sign

«What sign

«I just fell, and I just looked into some shoes

«Was that your sign, shoes

«Yes, it was

«What was that sign, you have never told me that

«I am going to tell you this, so you will understand that, that this call is different, it is real

«Tell me more

«Well those shoes was Nike shoes

«Yes, what about them?

«The motto to Nike is "just do it"

«That is true, but it is not based on facts

«Sometimes we have to make some decisions. True or not true?

«Yes, that is true, but I base my decisions on facts

«You use a horrible long time, to make decisions, sometimes the world moving fast, and then we have to follow our feelings. In most cases they are right, but we have to make a lot of time to convince other people that they are right

«But it makes our lives safe

«safe is true, but there are no action

«We are getting off the track, now

«I see too, where this is ending. I will continue on my story

«You are a nice peace maker sometimes

«The power of the man is great

«Sometimes you are right

«Well, back at the track. I was looking at those, shoes, and I told my self "What"

«Then, I just got it "Just to it"

«I told myself, but...but...but...

«Just do it. Hope you see, that tried to tell myself not to follow that sign, so the sign was repeated

«You are a funny man, my love

«So after that festival, I just meet one of the nerds at school. And I got an idea. I talked up to him, and told myself, I am going to tell him sorry and use him

«Use him, you are sometimes a really bad bad man, maybe I now understand why you failed

«I did not fail, it was just bad luck

She gives him a very big smile.

«Well I talked to him, told him sorry, and told him that I would make it god again. I told him that I know everything about finance and that I understand that he knows a lot about computers. He told me that he was making software. He said

«Free software

«That is why this world is going wrong, I told him. The greatest men in this world, one of the richest one is making and selling software, so maybe we can cooperate and make us rich, and be great men. In somehow, he agreed to that, but he was just a stupid nerd. I told him that if we make a good plan, we can borrow some money of my parents. Damn, how much I love that my parents money.

«Continue with your story

«Well, we worked very hard that summer, he had made some software that was doing something great, some sharing software

«That was nice

«I thought that was a stupid thought, but maybe it will work anyway. He made it finished, I didn't understand that software, but money was my idea. People get rich at software, really rich. We made a business plan, I talked to my dad, put a suite at the nerd, and we got money.

«Maybe you are an actor and can make a play one day

«I am a business man, We used the contact of my dad, to get a promotion.

«You where really high that time, you almost didn't have time to date me, but finally you asked me to marry me. That was so romantic you read me a poem

Please kindly marry
I am in a really hurry
I will not really bury

Take this expensive ring
The shining wonderful thing
Let the magic of gold sing

Into the future we walk
Into the future we talk
The future we will make

Please take this man
Hold him in your hand
He is sitting in the sand

«A man got to do, what he needing to do

«Everything was happiness that time

«Yes, it was, I just did it

«My company was going the right way. I got into the stock marked, we got rich

«Yes, we did

«I bought to everything

«You was the great man, thanks of buying me that gallery

«My parents laughed at me that time

«That was a great weeding gift, continue with the story

«The nerd worked very hard, with his software, to make it into to a selling product. Into boxes, wrapping is everything, branding the software. The stock made me a king. They was really waiting, the new big shot was coming. That is business, selling just an idea

«There you said it!

«What?

«It was just an idea, it was a great idea

«You forgot the product

«The stupid nerd, didn't make it. He put the product behind my back and published at Internet, he was working together with some people at Internet, sharing software

«Free software?

«Free software, yes, stupid nerd, we don't make money on free products, thats was my unlucky part.

«I think you was only thinking about money, money, money

«The art of money, it what makes this planet living

«Are you really shore about that?

«Are you kidding me?

«The result show how it went

«That was really bad bad luck, trusting that stupid nerd

«You was so young and naive

«No, it was bad luck, so my company went broke, when the marked got the news about that the product was at Internet, free

«What happened to the "stupid nerd"

«Well, someone from NASA, asked him to work for them, and he went to the desert, I think

«So your "stupid nerd" did make a living

«Yes, I did to, starting to write in that finance magazine

«Yes, you did, but it didn't make you happy. I am very happy that you are telling me the truth

«That is marriage, trust and truth

«I call it Yin and Yang, sweetie

«You are really talking codes my love. The nerd is still working at NASA

«Do you still have contact with him ?

«No, but I meet him yesterday at the restaurant

«I didn't see him

«He was there and just left before you arrived the restaurant

«That restaurant is so nice, I remember the first time, we went there

«You said, we can to inside there, because it doesn't fit my style

«But, you made it after all

«What did the nerd say

«Well he was in town, going to a meeting with some government people

«He was talking about the moon and that their was going to build something at the moon, making big plans

«I asked him what, but he told me that he could not tell me.

«I asked him if NASA have secrets, people owns the company, using my tax money

«Well, he said, ask the government. I am just the pianist

«I don't care as long, they use all my money on stupid projects

«maybe someone is thinking big

«If someone is thinking big, where is the money I told him.

«He didn't answer me, he just left

«So that was why I don't meet him, did he have the same look as back in collage

«What question is that? I do not care about looking

«That is for shore, your suite doesn't fit you stomach

«You are bad talking sometimes, but you love me, I am the unlucky boss, but I am going to show you this time.

She shows him a big big smile

«Time will show

«Let us make some dinner together

«What do we have in the electric magic box, the box of love ?

«I picked up some stuff, some green stuff

«Why do you do that, do I look like a cow, eating grass

«Have every seen a cow by the way, in real life

«No, but I have seen them at the TV

«Great, you can eat the TV, and I will make some salad and pasta

«You are funny to my dear, maybe I will survive the meal

They are walking to the kitchen, an makes the dinner together. It gets really nice looking, and they put it at their table. He gets a bottle of wine, red wine and she gets some candles, romance in partnership.

Planning the trip

After the dinner, they clean up, and makes some tea, heading to the sofa, The white one with a nice looking, like new fashion.

«How are you going to find Jesus, my love

«I don't know, but I thought if I was Jesus, I be in an other costume, than he had in the old days

«What costume?

«In the old days, he was walking in with clothes, looking like sheets putt around him, in colors of white, red and blue

«How do you know that?

«Have you ever been to a church?

«Yes, but what do you think about?

«In my old church there was a lot of pictures of him

«Just like photos

«Yes, just like photos

«Interesting, but how will the new Jesus look like.

«I just think that he will be modern. Staying at the beach, surfing like the the guys, at the east coast, be really cool, and in the evenings, he is sitting around in the fire playing his guitar and sing songs about God and salvation, maybe be making some prayers. Maybe the guitar is like a cross and his surfboard is tagged with painting of God.

«Did God tell you this?

«No, but I believe that I will get a sign, when I get there. I think he has got that guitar, just like a cross, really rocking dude.

«Well, you are funny, your signs are really great, maybe you could make me fairy tails one day.

«Come on, I don't have all the answers in this call, so you ask and I had to make up something. I will get a sign

«So is he in the Holy land?

«Yes, where else?

«Maybe he got kids, married, divorced and moved to an other country, like normal people

«Some chance I have to take. Since he is going to Mekka, I suppose that he starts in his own country, make a trip to a Muslim country, to convert to get into Mekka

«What do you know about Mekka

«My clever friend told me about Mekka

«Do you have a clever friend?

«You know that man who is going to calculate the perfect throw?

«Yes, he is nice

«Nice, do I nothing about, but clever he is. He told me that Mekka was placed in the center of the earth. Mekka is a holy place of the Muslims, every Muslim have to go to Mekka once in his lifetime, to be a true Muslim

«Yes, I have seen pictures from Mekka, it is like a stone, and a lot of people going around it. Really like ants.

«Yes, they are singing player to their God. that God is the same God as our God, just a different name.

«Now, are you making fairy tails, did he call you too?

«I really don't like your call, so that is why I am asking, I care about you and will make sure that you have a backup plan

«God will give me a sign

«Yeah, I would hope that I could believe you, like you believe in Jesus. make me and backup plan, if you don't find him, I need this plan before I will let you go

«Damn, please don't tell me that, the next thing you are going to ask after that is wearing a helmet.

«You great ideas seams to get out of control, so that is why I am have to make sure of the you will get back, if you get lost, I can't go down there and ask, have you seen a man looking for Jesus. He told me that he was going to the beach. Women have no rights in that country

«Well, I understand, where you are heading. So here is my plan. Tomorrow I will go to the church, and ask a priest about Jesus

«Don't you know that? You told me that your parents took you to the church.

«Well, in my younger days, I was playing Nintendo and listening to music at my mp3 player in the church

«Why did you do that?

«The priest was so boring, and my parents made me go to church

«Tell me more

«The priest just told, blahblahblah, let us pray....blahblahblah. Amen

«I understand, did you learn anything about angels

«They are white and have wings

«So he did not tell you about true angels, do you know anything about God then

«he is in heaven, sitting at a cloud

«Tell me more about you backup plan, I really have a bad feeling

«After I have talked to the priest and told him my call, he will believe me, he is a holy man, I will order an ticket to the holy land, then I will make a reservation of a hotel near the beach.

«Are you shore that that place is by the sea? Maybe it is at that holy wall. The sea is far away from the holy wall.

«Damn, you are an angel. Thanks my love

«I do that, I think God is talking threw you. You are my sign!

«Funny fairy tail man, you are

«Well tell me next step, in my backup plan, is looking in a Muslim country, maybe he has moved, tied of waiting of women making him to plan his whole life, a safe lifejacket.

«I suggest that you make a trip to a Muslim country that you know, and then make a ticket back to this city

«That is a good idea, my angel, my credit card is my salvation, and that is my true bible

«So you haven't read the bible?

«No, that is nerd stuff, it makes them silly

«So tell my why you think Jesus is going to Mekka

«Good point, Gods way are many, maybe Jesus is going to tell me the true story and ask me to write a book of his journey, when is is going to tell the people in Mekka that they are wrong and we are right. The truth!

«Maybe he can stop some wars?

«What wars?

«The holy wars, that has been going around all these years.

«We did not start that wars, they did, they doesn't know

«So are we better people than them?

«Yes, we are, we rule the world.

«What does you clever friend tell you about that?

«I have never asked him, he is my friend, and what I believe is my business and what he believes is his business.

«I think that all people are equal, and have the same rights in this world, so I will support your trip. Lets go to sleep, but can you do me a favor and read this book before you go to the priest.

«Why is that?

«Read it, and then ask, maybe I will be home early in the morning, if you start now.

«Damn, what about the match tonight, and I need some beers

«Well, do you want to make that trip or not ? If you do your trip without reading this book, you are at your own, in the rest of your life

«Wow, it seams that you really think that is the the best to do?

«I am not kidding with you?

«Sometimes, the boss is listening to his angel, so I'll start right away, Where is it ?

In the book shelf, in the working room.

«what is it called ?

«I will get it, so you not will get lost in the jungle of books, Maybe you realize that there are lot of books in the world and some of them are based on facts.

«Like learning books?

«Some are, but most of them are like, start to think your self, wrapped up in novels or a roman. As you said, what you believe is your business.

«That is right, but I will do a shoot, do my best

«Good night my sweetie, good reading night

«Well, I do something that I haven't done in years

«make me and summary, so you can tell me what did you learn

«I'll just catch up my helmet first, maybe the words are falling into my head.

The truth about Jesus

He started to read the book, but wonder how he is going to make an summary. He has not read any books in years, but he is a fast reader since he is a writer in that magazine. He starts to read the book, and find that there is already a summary in the book, and that this says that Jesus is the king of the Jewish people and that he lived after several years after his death. He suddenly realize that the whole thing was just an act, the Jesus act, someone just made up the story.

«No, I don't believe that, that is impossible

«Hiding the story for so, long, I really believed them, fake people fake people

«Where is the truth?

He trowed away the book, and started to watch TV instead. He was very upset and had to find a movie to watch instead. This movie is going to be interesting. It is the movie about Jesus Christ. While watching, he realized that the ending of the movie was a little strange, it was not like the whole movie. Maybe it was different, made on purpose, to tell this secret about Jesus. He fell asleep after the movie, in his chair and sleeps very heavy, that he doesn't wake up when she is going to work. He wakes up later that morning, and walks strait to bed, to get more sleep, he is worn-out, of all the information of the last day.

Final call

She is coming back from work and is in a happy mode, she has done it great. She had sold some photo art, a new artist that is going to be great, he signs his art with an writing like a president, very hard to tell the name, but pictures are amazing, so nice beautiful. The world is nice.

«So how was your day, my sweet little bunny. Hallo are you there. What is up? You look so sad?

«I got a call

«From whom

«I fell asleep and he called me again

«wow, that is really really great, what his he say, the great great father, this time

«wrong number

«ohhh, my dear, maybe you should, start listening to us

«What to you mean?

«The truth, angels my dear, angels

«Do you mean, that they exists

«There are a lot of them, some are very very special.

«Like you?

«No, my dear

«Code maker, there you are, I only see you, you are my true angel, I don't believe in anything more.

«Maybe, you could make a course or start read some books, since you now have a lot of time

«But what about money, the true art

«This has been a very good day, my dear, and there is going to be a lot more. People seems to like art better these days, than in the past. Maybe art is better than stocks. Maybe you can join me tomorrow

«Well, you are my angel, so why not, my world is turned upside down anyway.

«Well first we are going to rest

«Rest, my world has explode

«Maybe I can make you a man, read me the poem, whisper it into my ear

«You are an true angel, make a sad sad man, into happy man, just like that

«Well are we going to rest

«You bet! Secrets, secrets, secrets or what?

«Did you, make a summary

«I haven't finished the book, it was too complicated to read.

«Please read the book finished and make my some words

«I will make it like a poem

«What do you mean

«I got codes to, my love

«Write me, write me, but first rest.

They are heading to the bedroom, and the next days he works very hard to read the book, and he makes a lot of notes, putting them into an order. She is going to work as usual and they have their normal routines as they have, in the past, the moods are happier and the magic power of love is sounding their environment. After some days, he is ready of his poem.

«My angel, I am finished, he tells from the working room. I will clean up, and read it to you

«Great, I am very exited

«I will be right there, driving my limousine, do you have the red carpet ready

«Yes, my dear, the fantasy carpet is just in place.

He is coming out of the office and taking place in the sofa. She puts away her book, and is ready to listen

«The poem is called, Jesus walked to Mekka, in rhythm poetry, and goes like this

I am just a WRITER

Maybe an angel FIGHTER
Doing the FATHER act
That is the FACT

I am just a TEACHER

Maybe a nice PREACHER
To all the CHILDREN of the LIGHT...
Yes, that is RIGHT, let us FIGHT

We can not WAIT

The CANDLES have to burn
The PURPLE candles
They are KILLING them self

JESUS went to heaven

That was the TIME of seven

Mohammed went MEKKA

Maybe he had seven SHAKRA

Maybe he had found the KEY

Someone ACT to let him die

Someone in ROME was afraid

That taxes NOT he PAID

He was the KING

As Martin LUTHER king

Let us wonderful SING

That is the real THING

«That was really strange, why do you use big letters some time, and some times not

«That is the code, my love, I will tell you how the code is

«Please do that, I will make some notes, just wait, I am running like hurricane to get something.

«Bring the laptop, we can write it into the poem right away

«Working together in harmony is great, we are a great team

«A small powerful team, I know why God made us getting together, we fill into the empty spaces, that is missing

«You are clever, finally you understand, tell me the poem, maybe one day you will mediate and not hesitate

«Damn is it a poem, not business, may be you can write a poem yourself

«Working together is better, cooperation is humanity, like we to together with my friends. Tell me the poem, my dear

I am just a WRITER

He means that Jesus was telling things and writing things philosophy like Mohammed.

Maybe an angel FIGHTER

He was fighting against the men of power, the priests and the people in Rome

Doing the FATHER act

He was married and did it to support the children of the world

That is the FACT

He wrote it in the Jesus documents

I am just a TEACHER

He was telling the world something how to live

Maybe a nice preacher
he was speaking to the people

To all the CHILDREN of the LIGHT...
To the people that is bright

Yes, that is RIGHT, let us FIGHT

He wanted it to be right, so he did the act as a theater

We can not WAIT

He had to speak to the people now, that was his mission in life

The CANDLES have to burn

Priest are just talking in churches

The PURPLE candles
Priest often use the color purple in their clothes, thinking that they are the people who tells the truth, but Jesus was using colors of write, blue and red. He uses astrology, stars and planets.

They are KILLING them self

Priest are going to make this world as a payback time, more and more people do not believe in Christ, people are becoming the knowledge

JESUS went to heaven

Jesus died several years after his death, about fifty years

That was the TIME of seven

A Pope in the 1600 age, made the world, following the clock and not the heart, people likes to work, helping each other for a living, making a better place to live, Working together, not against each other

Mohammed went MEKKA

Mohammed was also a prophet, like Jesus, he changed the city of Mekka into a better place to live. There was a lot of bad people before, drinking and killing.

Maybe he had seven SHAKRA

People that meditate, are able to place their minds into a another world. He was learning fast, from the angels and the souls in the other world, it is codes, colors and signs. These people know the future, because life is a contract, the soul.

Maybe he had found the KEY

Shakra is also used in in Buddhism, high monks and the Maya priests, end the priest in Egypt, Faraoes was traveling by light, the soul

Someone ACT to let him die

The killing of the crucify, was almost killing him

Someone in ROME was afraid

Rome wanted him away

That taxes NOT he PAID

He didn't follow the rules of Rome, pay money, he didn't like money

He was the KING

He was the true king of the Jude's

As Martin LUTHER king

He was talking about life, he was not afraid to die, he know his future.

Let us wonderful SING

the Koran is 115 songs, telling people how to live, easy to understand of people that does not know how to read, people remember a song, not a hole book. It is mostly following your heart, be kind, share, build together, don't be envy, take care of your wifes and the children, the soul is reflected in the eyes.

That is the real THING

This is the truth

Truth cannot be changed, but truth can be hidden.

«You are wonderful man, maybe he told you more that you understand, you are becoming a man, that is why I married you

«I got no call, today, just a joke, he told me, so that is why I read the book, and went into Internet and learned more. This is just like reawakening, opening a new world, thinking bigger. Maybe the soul of Jesus, went into Mohammed, who knows, maybe he next Jesus is able to tell, if he is able to look into this past life's, just a thought, why not?

«May I can learn to meditate and join your world to, let us play some cards, first

«Cards like poker, I finished that a years ago, I was easy, but boring

«These are tarot cards

«These strange cards, are they true to

«Maybe, if we read them right

«Tell me more about them

«They are like telling the future, they are from northern Italy, maybe from Islamic Egyptian times. Making a man into connection of the cosmos, the creator, like in alchemy.

«Show me some of these cards

«I made an expert make them to you

«To me?

«Yes, long time ago, and they where amazing

«So you knew all the time, this was going to happen

«Yes, I did, but I didn't know when. Destiny has no clock, it follows the clock of the universe.

«What is that?

«I am not shore, but the Maya people is telling something about time, 1618 is going to change back to 1320.

«Maybe I can calculate that one day. Mekka is in earth positions 1618, the perfect number.

«Your cards are The Wheel of Fortune Card, The World Card, The Pope Card

«We don't have three cards in poker, so one of them must be a joker

«The wild cards, unbeatable, my superman

Joy and sorrow
is not anything we borrow
When we are unhappy
Someone is to bossy
Bad treated within our soul
Making us not whole

Joy and sorrow
It is when we are happy
It is like a sweet candy
Within our soul
Making us whole

Bed time stories

Later in the evening, they are heading to bed, the bedroom has really changed atmosphere. It is just like, the colors of aura has changed. Colors like, white, blue and red are flowing in the air. Magic invisible light, that is not able to be seen. Maybe the pictures has got a new meaning. Telling the stories of the pictures and just not colors and brush touches that has made wonderful hand work.

«Well, what are you going to do now

«I don't really now

«Maybe you can do me a favor

«What is that?

«Make you trip to the holy land, write a book about the truth, study some pictures in the holy land

«Well I have the tickets and some money, so why not

«and I really need to change my life and make listen to you

«maybe a pilgrim travel is needed

«I am going to miss you very much, my angel

«I will always be in your heart, you are a really nice man

«I do my best, I am changeable and do everything for you

«everything?

«yes, behind a large man the is always a clever woman

«so will you make me a child

He get silent and is just looking at her, with an empty look. She know that he is thinking and she gets a little bit upset and asks him

«well

«well?

«Yes, I will do that, but who is going to take care off that child, while you are at work

«You mentioned everything!

«Damn, I really need a pilgrim trip, maybe I can learn something about people

«World is nice, go out and talk to them, learn them, then you will grow and make your self the best man in the world and be a real hero. Just like superman!

«I really need a vacation, this to much information, I have been working really hard, in the last days

«Great idea, but I have to work with, making us a living

«But I need it

«Make your own trip, make it to holy land

«No way, I am going to have a vacation in that country, full of lies

«The are some, nice trips to northern Africa, relax at the beach and maybe later we can go to a nice place, Let me play you some music first so we can dance, dance into the future, future of love, that will only grow

«Maybe I will bring the laptop

«Please do that, write some fantasy stories of your mind

«What?

«Be in the story, just write, you are wonderful crazy, no rules. Only heart rules

«I will do my best, my white angel

«I am always with you, in you soul, my dear

Children is when we use true love
That will we show, To our create humans
In bodily commons, In deep commitment
and great movement

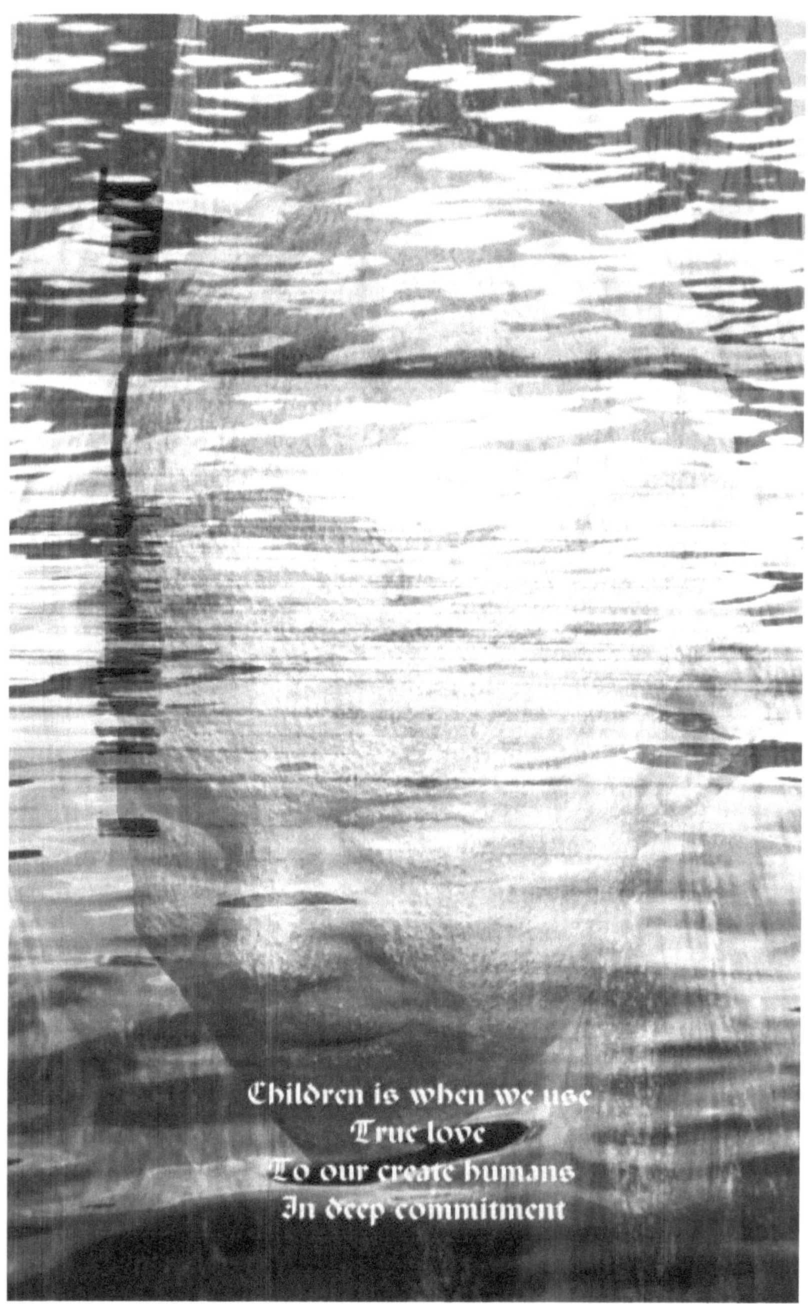
Children is when we use
True love
To our create humans
In deep commitment

The mentor

He is living in a small apartment, just enough to him self, and of having the visit of his kid and other relatives. The apartment is located in the city, not to far from his work, making him able to walk to and from the office. Two bedrooms and a nice living room, and a hall separating the room. The living room is covered with some shelves, with books and some pictures of his kid and family. He has got a big flat screen TV, with a surround system attached. The phone is calling, he is wondering, if why he left the mobile phone in the hall, but he gets up of his chair and walks to the hall, and picks the phone out of the pocket in his leather jacket.

«Hi, Jack, how are you doing?

«Fine thanks!

«I am really great to, I got fired last week

«Fired and you are happy about that ?

«Yes, I am going to write books instead

«That seems to be nice. I like books and movies. What are you going to write about ?

«That is a secret

«So you are calling me to tell, about nothing? What is the secret?

«I am going to tell you more later on, do you have time for a lunch tomorrow

«Lunch?, that was a new one, are you drunk? Just kidding with me ?

«Ohhh, no, I am starting a new life, a happy life

«Have heard about some of you life project before, so why not. They are really funny, I agree about that you are becoming a book writer, because your fantasy is really big, sometimes. Have you talked about this with your wife ?

«Yes, and she agrees

«Well, she is really nice, so I am happy to you, lets meet tomorrow at lunch. Do you know my regular restaurant, not far from my work ?

«Yes, I do, when do you have time ?

«Is one o'clock fine ?

«That is great, see you tomorrow, take care so long

«Take care you too, Carl

He hangs up the phone, and really wounder about what he was up to.

Getting fired and that happy ? Strange, I wish that he had told me more.

He gets back to his TV, and is trying to find a movie, to get him relaxed. He had worked really hard in the latest days, the project he is working on, is going to be presented to the management next week, and that is going to made him able to going live with his work in the autumn. The project is going into practical phase.

He is not able to concentrate to look at a movie today, so he is stepping out in the balcony to get some fresh air, before he is getting into his bed and making his hours of sleep, so that he can enjoy a new day at work, with his project team. The spring is in the air, he can smell the fresh air of the trees outside in the backyard. The small leaves of the trees are getting bigger and bigger of each day, almost getting out of the cocoon that they have been locked up into in the past months. He really enjoys the spring, it is like making a new beginning, everything is born again in the nature, trees are getting green, flowers of all different colors are getting up, grass getting greener, making people happy. Every season has is charm, winter with snow, soft crystals coming from the sky, summer with heat, making our bodies warm and comfortable, autumn with colors, leaves that flows gently in the wind, coloring the world we see, and maybe looking forward to get into your houses with warm and safety before the storms and the winter is heading into our life's.

He is very happy to live in this apartment, having some green space to make him feels that he lives not to far from the nature, and still living in the city. He really doesn't understand how Carl and his wife Maria is able to live in that tall building, just made of glass and steel, but inside the apartment is really nice. She is really a good designer, but she works with art, to she has got really nice taste, she knows how beauty is looking and has the feeling of beauty. He has always wonder, what she see in Carl, he is a very strange and witty man, but at the same time, he is regular, maybe it is the funny part that she likes. It have always been something special about them, they are like connected in some way, even if they are so different. Maybe that is the thing, the difference.

I the apartment of Carl and Maria, which is located in a modern building in the city center. The building is covered with glass, dark glass, almost looking like a business building. There are a guard in the ground floor, and they are living in the tenth floor. The apartment has two bedrooms, a living room with integrated kitchen and a hall. One of the bedrooms are a office, and they have no children. He is not in a rush, he wants to have a stable job, he hasn't been to lucky about that in his life. She is working at a gallery, she is a manager of the gallery and doing well. The apartment is in a modern style with wooden floors and black furnishers, there are a lot of pictures, but that is not surprising since she is working at a gallery.

Carl returns from the working room, with a big smile

«Did it go well my dear?

«Yes, it did, Maria

«You always use my name, when you are happy, so I trust you about that is went well. Did you tell him ?

«I just told him that I was fired and that I would like a lunch tomorrow

«What did he say about that ?

«You, know we men don't talk to much about things like that we just give a message and then we are finished, right on target. But I could hear that he was very surprised, he asked me if I was drunk

«That was not surprising, because you have really changed in these last days, you are full of energy again, haven't seen that for a long time.

«I feel whole, and that is thanks to you, made me discover that maybe I am a writer, a book writer.

«You are a writer, you have been writing all the time in you last job, at that newspaper and you are witty, so that is why I want you to be a book writer. You have a talent, and if you let you self out, you can be a very nice writer.

«Thanks, I am very lucky to have you as my life partner, giving me all this support

«That is what I call a relationship, sicking together in good day and bad days. If a am having bad days, you are making me happy to

«Maybe, maybe not, I am always trying the best, I will never loose you, you are my angel

«You are so sweet

«Sometimes I have feelings to

«Yes, you have, you have a lot of them, you just not express them to much, hope that writing will loose you up a bit more, really getting know of your self.

«Life is hard out there, in the city, living is not easy.

«Agree about that, maybe the world is changing one day, when be are becoming aware of it.

«What do you mean about that ?

«That is what you are going to learn, when you travel to Italy, hope that your friend will join you. He is interested in art, so why not, I think will will be happy when you ask him, just stay on the ground, so he doesn't think that this one of your crazy ideas, that you never do. I just say good luck and have a nice travel, because you are doing this to both of us. Making this relationship going into the right direction, maybe we can afford a vacation together one day, when you have published some books

«Some books, I am going to be the best writer in the world, with my first book

«I just say, stay on the ground, I will stay home, and watch out of the money, so long, and remember, you don't know yet, when your friend is available. Maybe there will be several weeks, before you are able to do that trip.

«That will be fine, I have a lot of homework to do, I will do that trip even if he is not able to do it.

«I just think that you need someone to travel with you, because you will maybe be learning a lot of him, he is quit different than you think, I know him we have talked a lot in these parties we have had. Maybe he is a little bit sad, inside, because he is single. Everyone wants a partner.

«Not all want that, many people is happy living alone.

«I know that, but these people are living with other family or friends.

«Sometimes you have to open you eyes, the are a lot of people living alone in the city. People dies of aloneness.

«That is not my problem, they can just be friends with everyone is they like

«Maybe they not feels strong like you

«I am not strong

«Yes, you are. You never give up, that is a great side of you, if you meet a closed door, you just try another.

«Sometimes you win and sometimes you loose, that is just way of living

«And you have a great positive thinking, always heading forward. Many people doesn't understand what you are doing, so they think you are far away, making to big plans in your life. Sometimes I am thinking that I am happy that you not have money, because you would always be going up and down with your projects. Mostly down, but becoming a writer is a great idea.

«Thanks

«I will go to bed now, will you enjoin me?

«I am going to do some more research, making some plans of the trip, so go ahead, I will catch up later, and I suppose that you will be reading anyway, and you are complaining about that I am getting to sleep to fast.

«Good night, and have good luck tomorrow, hope that he will join you.

She gives him a kiss and is heading to the bathroom, and he is heading to the office. He works a lot and heading to the bedroom late in the night, and he look at her with a sweet smile and thinks he is the luckiest man on the world.

Carl is entering the restaurant a little bit earlier, and he is looking around, to see if he is able to find his friend. One of the waitress, is looking at him and asks

«Do you want a table ?

«Yes, please! I was looking for a friend, he is maybe coming later. Maybe you know him, he is one of your regular customers

«How does he look like

«He use to have a suite, loose fitted, not tie. A little bit taler than me, dark hair

«That seems to be just exactly like everyone of my regular customers, there are a lot of offices around here.

«Well, well, I will drop by the empty table at the window so long, he will show up. Give me a coup of coffee so long.

«Right away, mister

He takes place at the table, the restaurant, is regular as they all look, not of the cheapest one type, but a cheap one in the business area. He looks out the window and looks at the people that is walking heading somewhere. He wonder where they are walking, maybe to their office or maybe to a meeting, mostly of these people are carrying a briefcases, some of them are carrying backpacks.

«Your coffee, mister

«Thanks

He was waked up of his thinking, and the smell of fresh coffee reaches him. He looks at the cup and the cup is telling him that the heat is to high, to drink it right away. He picks up a notepad of his jacket and reads some of his notes, to prepare him of his meeting with his friend.

«Hello Carl

«Oh, hey Jack

Jack finds the chair opposite of him and drops of his jacket in the neighbor chair and places him self in soft and firmly in the chair.

«Have you ordered?

«No, I just go a cup of coffee so long, you business people are hard to tell when to come.

«That is a new one, you are always late

«As I told you I have started a new life

«Lets order first and then tell me more, if you first starts talking, then you are way of into fantasy land.

«You are always so practical, lets order

Carl picks up the menu, and looks it in short time, found his choice. He looks at Jack and he turns around to get in contact with one of the waitress. The woman that showed him his table comes by and smiles

«You should told me that he was the cute guy, she saids

«How can I tell you that, I don't look at men like you do, Carl says

«Are you ready to order, I guess you want the regular, Jack

«Yes please, he says

«And you, mister

«I want a hamburger and a coke

«Right away, she says and moves quickly back to the kitchen

«She really likes you, Jack

«Yes, she does, we have a good tone

«Why don't you date her?

«No, we are just like friends

«That is nice, but you knows that she really likes you

«Friends doesn't do that, and I am not the type who wants that, you know that, look at your self, you are a very lucky guy that has Maria

«You are right, we are same type of personality, in that way

«You are right about that, else you are flying like everywhere, and I am staying at the ground. Tell me about getting fired, I was wondering a lot about that, why you where so happy

«The thing is that I had a project in my mind for some time, and this gave me an opportunity to get ahead with that project. Just an kick start.

«What did Maria, say about that? Your project?

«Well I kind of landed, but we are kind of working together, so I have changed it, and going to write about something else

«About what ? I am not really shore, but it is maybe, about life

«That seems to be a serious book, life is serious

«That is the thing, I am going to write about life in a positive way, a happy life, ups and downs, but newer giving up, go ahead with your dreams.

«That seems to be an good idea, here comes our food

The waitress is placing the food in front of them and says

«Enjoy, misters

«Thanks, they both says, and getting ready to, go on with the food

«Hey, Jack, what is that ?

«What?

«Is that food, this is real food

«My body don't need so much, so I go light, much food get me lazy at work.

«Soup and salad is not food of a man

«But I am working with people, not physical stuff, I am sitting a lot of all my day at my work, tell me more about your book project

«Just a minute, I am going to finish my meal, and then I can talk, tell you my plans

«Yes, nice

They stay quite and finish their meals, Carl is a fast eater and Jack is more like enjoying the meal, in pleasure. Jack is more of that type, eating quality food and Carl is eating to feed his body.

After finishing the meat, they order some coffee.

«So, what is your plans Carl ? He asks interesting, during he is holding his cup of coffee between his hands.

«I plan to go to Italy to do some research, my first plan I had to drop, there was to many holes in my story, so I had to change it, and Maria asked me to write about Italy, because she has a dream about going there and she said, why don't you write about Italy, the are so many people that dreams about that country, especially women, in the romantic way, but men like that country too, buildings, and like you art. I like buildings, architecture.

«Don't forget, wine and fast cars and fashion. And the nature of Italy is amazing.

«yes, you have been traveling around in Europe in the last years.

«yes, that is true, I have been to Spain, Paris in France and Rome in Italy, short trips. I like art, it gives me different input to my life, my job is working with people, so vacations to me is nature and art.

«I heard about Rome, some guys where talking about is, do you know what they said.

«No, tell me

«I asked them is they have seen the pope, and of of them told me, I didn't see the pope, may he is taking some dope, hanging in a rope, I hope. Then another guy said we don't want him to be hanging around. Maybe he is just waving with his stick, because he is very sick.

«You are funny, I guess your retelling is different than the real story, that is I am very happy to hear, that you are going to write. You have a good fantasy, and are a good teller. A you know how to write.

«Thanks, Jack, you are a really different person, when we talk together, just me and you.

«Life has a lot of sides. Enjoyable sides, making our life rich, input from different sides.

«Agree about that, I just have forgot to live, that is why I need to start a new life, or maybe go back to live the life I forgot.

«Nice to hear

«What is your plan for vacation this summer

«Haven't decided yet, I have been working a lot, with a big project at work. It have taken all my attention.

«Maybe you need a vacation

«Everybody needs a vacation sometimes. I am asking you to join me to north Italy, traveling like friends, you like to read books, so you can help me give me input of the book, I don't know so much about traveling and art, so I ask you to join me, I will pay the expenses, and traveling with a friend is nice, and maybe we learn about more each other and become real nice friends.

«That is nice, but I have to think about that one

«But, you never been to Milan and Venice ?

«No

«Do you want that ?

«Have been thinking about that, but have always been thinking, that I am going there later, if I a get a woman on day. A really nice woman.

«maybe you will meet her in Italy

«I don't think so, but I will think about you invitation. I am going to present my project plans of the management of the company next week, and can make some plans after that. Time is running, I have to go back to work. Someone is working

«hey, writing is a lot of work to

«I know, just kidding, I have been writing a lot of project plans and report in my life. Lot of research.

«Thanks, you are funny to, if you want

«Life is enjoyable

«I pay the lunch, go back to your work, do your work, and we will talk next week.

«I really like your plan, write me more details in a mail. I will look at it and decide.

«I will do that, boss! I will work hard! See you in Italy!

Giving is when we share

What we want to dear

Our recourses with other

Like that you are my brother

Without having anything in return

And not in a pattern

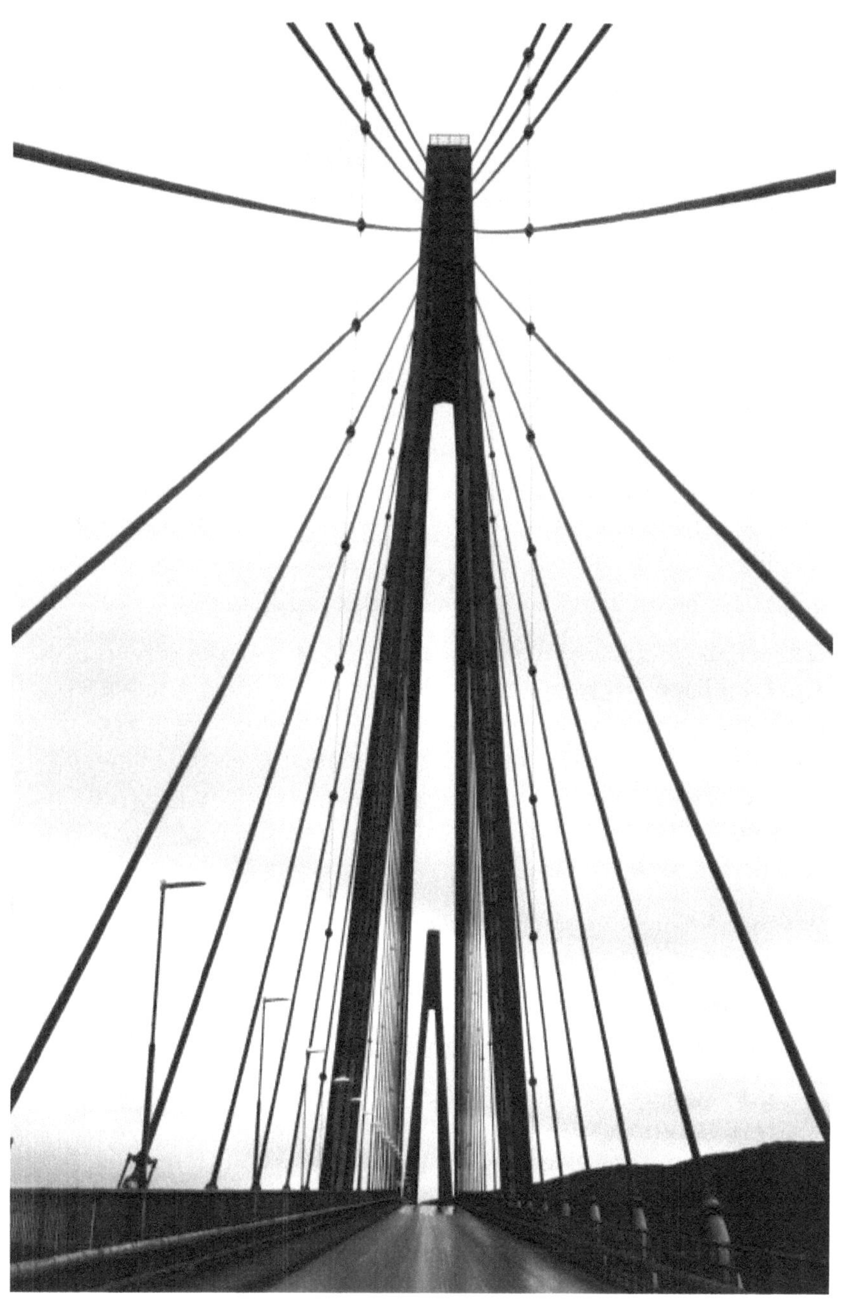

Arriving Milan

Some month later, the where arriving Italy, they travel to London and changed flight to Milan. Carl was looking out the window, in the minutes before they landed, watching the mountains. The Alps was really amazing, these mountains was climbing towards these clouds, they looks like cotton, flowing kindly in the air. The top of the mountains are covered with show, almost looking like sugar, just like someone had put sugar one these rocky mountains, that is separating Europe. The airplane, is diving into into the clouds and hunting of the airport that is firmly on the ground, making them safe on the ground. The landing of the airplane made people breathing again, even if the pilot landed it in gentle maneuverer, soft and steady.

«I am very happy that you said yes to this trip, Jack

«That is just a pleasure. I will get a lot of new experience out of this trip. I am happy to travel with you because you are a funny friend, and I enjoy that, that is really vacation to me, work is serious. I have been working very hard, and the management liked my plans and told me, reload your batteries, Jack and we see you in the Autumn, maybe this company will survive thanks to you, is is going to be though, but we will make it.

«Work have to be like that, serious, people don't trust us we are just joking around.

«That is right, and let us have some fun times in this trip, I am going to write a book when I am home, this is just a holiday research fun trip

They got their baggage, they are traveling with only one suitcase each, the trip is easier that way, and they are lucky to be men traveling, needing a lot of things they not need like women do, they need a lot of things to look beauty like TV and magazines tell them to look.

Carl looks out the window, during the trip to the city, to the center of Milan. The nature is covered with industrial building like other cities he had been visiting, he really hopes that this city is different, he had seen a lot of pictures, and this is how this city is presented, but Milan is a big industrial and administration center, together with business, culture, art, fashion and design.

«Cars are different here, Carl says

«Welcome to Italy, my friend, home of fast cars, in nice design

«Yes, right, maybe we can see a lot of Ferrari's, in the center of the city, filled with spaghetti western, raiding around in a horrible speed.

«I know why Maria, asked you, to ask me, someone need to organize you, you would have got lost in you fantasy.

«And I am very happy to travel with you my friend, because is I have traveled with Maria everything just had to so romantic, now we can be men, practical, going to the goal, be focused, don't think about everything, not planning everything,. Drink when we want, not having someone telling us, don't drink to much, be careful, watch out of the bad guys and so one, and so one, and so one, and so one

«You are right about that. Remember we are here to see Italy, this is not going to be a party. This is a different culture, and I want to respect that. We are tourists.

«I am an undercover agent, disguised as an tourist, writer on holiday, making my notes about the secret Italy, why are everybody going to this country, or why does everybody go to this country. I am going to hunt people, the soul of the Italians.

«I am going to say at the ground, maybe look at some art.

They are arriving the train station, Carl is very impressed about it. I am in Italy, the real Italy. He feels the soul of Italy. The station had a got a great bow, where the trains arrive, covered with glass and marble stones in at the floor and the walls. It is late in the evening, the temperature is high, and the air is moisten, making them sweat, and the clothes are sticking to their bodies.

«Lets get a cab, Jack

«I think it is that way, says Jack.

«After you, sir, lead the way, I am in the wind of what you say, replies Carl

Jack, really smiles, his friend is very funny, and he tells words like they are dancing, in a funny way. They find a cab and gets to the hotel. The hotel is not far away, just some minutes away from the station. Carl is paying, with a Euro note, he has picked up at the airport.

«Nice hotel, Carl

«Thanks, my intuition told me to stay at this hotel, Hotel Demidoff, almost like the sound and smell of cigars.

«What ? Jack is looking questioning at him

«Davidoff is a brand of cigars

«Great intuition, you got, Carl, maybe the next hotel is called hamburger or beer.

«Thanks, of trusting my intuition.

«I know about intuition, we use it a lot at work, but the difference is that we are documenting, our thoughts, so that other people can really on what we telling. People are different, management needs, facts to make their decisions.

«Leave your work home, we are on vacation.

Management is about taking care
Of what other human resources share
That is right leadership made clear
And the is reasonable be fair

They get checked into the hotel and agree going out for a beer, after some minutes of relaxing. They went to the bar that is located next to the hotel, after asking the receptionist where to go. The receptionist doesn't really understand what they are asking about, it seems that he doesn't understand what they are asking about, because the meaning of a bar, is quite different that they are used to. It is more like an fast food restaurant, but more like Italian style. The purpose of the travel was not to archive, what they have home so they are getting a beer before they are heading back to the hotel, they are tired after a long travel, sleeping at a airplane is not the same as sleeping in a soft bed.

The next day Carl wakes up and is fresh, and ready to get into the life of this city. He walks to the window and put the white curtains and the brown shutters away from the window, that has hold the shining morning sun away from the room. He wants to shout out load "God morning, Milan" in a tone like the old sentences "God morning Vietnam". He thinks that is not the right place, because while he gets he fresh sun in his body, he realized, that he is staying in a wonderful place. The street is covered with houses that are painted in white and light yellow colors, and there are a lot of marble balconies surrounding these apartments. He gets exited and heads to the phone, and is dialing 424

«Hello, a tiered voice is answering

«Good morning, Jack, are you awake

«Good morning, Carl, no, I am sleeping, this is my answering machine, I always carry with me to answer intelligent questions , while I am sleeping.

«Sorry about that, but the world is waiting for us to be discovered, get down from your 737 room and lets get some breakfast

«Give me thirty minutes, and see you downstairs, and I live in room 424

«I know I just think 737 is a more funny number, like an airplane, full of speed, we are one a travel, time is to be enjoyable, sleep can be done in the next life. See you in thirty minutes and shower of your sleeping tone. Weather forecast of the day is sun, sun, sun, hot, hot hot, I have just looked out the window.

«Sleep well?

«Yes, until you rang

«See you, bye

Carl hangs up the phone, and steps into the shower and sings some songs. The bath room is covered with Italian tiles, making it pleasant and enjoyable. He is in a really happy mode.

Jack and Carl enters the breakfast room at the same time, and finds a empty table, a table covered with pink and white cloth. As a regular breakfast room at a hotel, the are tables with food, and a waitress is heading to their table.

«Bonjourno

«Bonjourno, duble espresso, Jack says

«Coffee, please, says Carl

She heads back to get their orders

«So, you are not quite living like a Italian, Jack replies

«What ? Carl replies

«They drink espresso in country, Jack replies

«This is my first day in Italy, can't learn everything at the same time. But you are my master, so I will learn, I am going to study you and all of the other people during this stay. The is one of my secret missions, at this trip

«Secret missions

«Not so load, please, people maybe understands American. Just kidding, I have something that I am going to study during the trip, writers do that. I have made a study at home, while you where working, and Maria have given me some input.

«And what is that ?

«I am going to tell you more about it, I am going to show you a world that people are not aware of. Later on my friend, and take more of this sticky sugar, that almost tastes like jam. The color maybe tells us what it is supposed to be.

«Agree to that, Carl

«Lets finish of this breakfast and head fast of the goals of the day, ready for walking. First we are going to hunt Dumbo

«I guess that you mean, Duomo

«Yes and no, maybe it is both, tell you later when we get inside. Are you ready for take off, I am going to fly like the winds of hurricanes.

«I am just going to get my camera, and then I am ready, meet you in the lobby about 10 minutes.

«I'll be there, my master

Jack steps out on the street as long, and looks across the road. He is watching a tobacco store, and heads to is, he is in Italy, so cigarillos are going into his pocket. He is going to be a man of Italian style. Maybe writers have to smoke a lot, because in the movies he has seen, writers always smokes, or maybe these movies was a kind of old. He just goes for the feeling, taste of small cigars, that smells like men. Later he returns back to the hotel, where Jack is waiting.

«I just had to catch up some smelling fresh air. Nice camera you go there, you look like a photographer

«It is just an ordinary camera, to people takes pictures.

«I don't know that world, hope to get some copies, when we get home.

«Yes, you will

«Maria, will be happy too

«I think Maria will be more happy than you

«You are right, I live in the world of words

«Maybe you can look at the pictures when you are home, and write what you see.

«That is nice, good idea. Now lets head to the main street and in the direction of the Duomo, Church of the churches. It is famous, have I read somewhere in my study.

«Lets have a look, show me the way, lead on

«Right on the target, I got a GPS

«That is new to me, they are nice to have in cars, but never tried it on the street

Carl taps on the screen and shows the way of direction. The GPS is telling with a voice where to go. They are heading right at the corner and then goes straight ahead.

«Watch you walking, Carl

«What ?

«You are to occupied with looking at that thing, your GPS, you have to look where we are, at the people with its surroundings. Maybe you are going to hit somebody, Where are we now ?

«This box tells me that we are just right here. Look

Carl stops and show the screen to Jack, with a face that is telling, let me tell you.

«You are becoming a writer, so tell me what is telling you

«It says, the are several hotels around us, a lot of restaurants and a monument right head of us.

«Nice, I can see the restaurants, we have passed lot of them, people are sitting there and enjoying food and life of company. Maybe friends. What is that monument ?

Carl taps at the screen, several times

«It doesn't say anything, stupid box

«Agree to that

«I got your point, maybe I should put it into my pocket, and we should use the map and the book I have got instead.

«Lets to that, that is living, in the place and not the virtual world. Let us go across the street and look at that monument, may there a a sign at it. Watch out these cars, they are fast running

«You are right about that, Italian drivers are stressed, they got great temper I have heard.

«They are famous

They walks to the monument, it is placed middle of a roundabout, or it probably more like they have build a roundabout the monument. There is a sign at the monument telling it is Port to Venezia.

«This is great, really nice, if we go that direction, we are going to be wet, because it is the road to Venezia, Carl replies

«Nice, but we are not going to the beach today, beaches are around the world everywhere, we are in Milan

«Amazing Milan, the statue is Athena, she is looking into into that direction. She is from the Greek mythology, wisdom and peace is covering hear

«Didn't know you where so wise, Carl

«I learned something at school, and refreshing my memory with this book, look the is Neptune to, is looking to Venezia too or maybe he is looking to Atlantis to city that went down into the oceans.

«You have great fantasy, let us stay in Milan, for some days and then you can walk in you fantasy land later on, when we are heading into that direction.

«You are right, Dumbo is waiting, let walk, follow me, I am going to use my old teachings from childhood, looking at the sun and the watch, then I know where north, east, south and west is, I am killing my machine and walking into the land of maps, paper is still useful, in these digital world.

«Maybe you are going to talk again

«Can't walk and talk at the same time, we are men, that is impossible woman tells us, but we are at our own now, so I will do my best. Lets walk

They are walking ahead, Carl has changed again, and becoming out of the box, more like living and happy, as they walk to the center of this city, the city covered with fashion, design and art.

After walking a long time, passing a lot of famous fashion stores they are heading into a piazza, with a outdoor café and a small church. The the opposite there are some fashion shops, and while they are looking into the blue sky, with the shining sun, they are able to see the Duomo behind these marble buildings.

«This heat is killing me, says Carl, lets make a break and enjoy the people that are passing by, people seems to be in a hurry, just like home, wonder where they are going in that speed.

«Not all people are at a vacation. Let gets into that café.

They are taking place at one of the empty tables, there a lot of them, and shade is covering the tables with big sun umbrellas. The is a calm in the air, making them happy, and they are ordering some espresso and water. They are really calm and looking at people that is passing by. Most of them are in business suites and dresses, but there are some people that are tourists.

«Did you see that man, Jack, that with a lot of heavy words inside his body?

«What?

«The man in the black suite, with mauve shirt and that white ring abound his neck, he was in a really hurry, and walk with firm steps into that office. That body is full of important words, a lot of them, they are nearly coming out of his skirt.

«I see what what you are heading to

«He was looking at us, with eyes that told me, give me room, I am in important business, big words are going in and out of my office at this church, and I have a lot of them, so I have to carry a pilot suitcase.

«I know, I know, if you continue to eat like you do back home, you will look just like him.

«I starting a new life, so maybe I am going to change diet to, people around here is not like home. Maybe Italian diet is better

«Are you hungry ? Replies Jack

«Nope, this heat is making me, only think about water, water water

«Let us pay, and continue to the Duomo, I am exited to look at you Dumbo.

They pay, and leaves the piazza, that has made them I a nice harmony with the surrounding of the Italian soul of this city. They are going strait ahead to the Duomo, in silence and with firm steps, like hunting for a goal, maybe a task of the day. Streets are covered with tiles made of stone, in the last part of the walk, making a like a red carpet into the Piazza de Duomo, with is surrounding the amazing cathedral, made in several hundreds of years. It shines like sculpture and is made of marble, stone of the soul of Italy. Jack is really amazed of the building and is making a lot of pictures, before they are walking to the main door.

«Got any bombs, Jack, better drop them of before we are going to fight those people, they seems to be scary

«Didn't know that you was scared of anything

«They got guns

«Hopefully that is just a symbol of power, showing a gun is that

«But I don't like them, these men are scaring me, and I don't like guns at all, peace and love in my heart, Imagine all the people......

«Right

«Well, let us get into the line, if you have dropped all the bombs and guns

«Don't joke about that, maybe they think are are crazy, they are doing a great job, protecting this building of art.

«Agree to that, this building is art, lets see what is inside, I got a mission

They are getting into the line and getting fast through the security control. They walk into the Cathedral, and are looking around, Jack looks at the paintings, Carl looks at the people, until he stop and looking at the wall. Jack steps up to him and asks, with a silent voice.

«What?

«Dumbo!

«Isn't that an angel

«Yeah, I am going to tell you more about it later, at lunch maybe, lets walk out, I don't like the painting of the men with great words telling us what is right and what is wrong. All people are nice people in my eyes.

«The art is nice

«Maybe, I don't know, I just look at these men, but the painting of Maria, I like.

«Lets walk outside

«Agree to that

They look at some of these paintings at their way of to the piazza, and stays in the large amazing piazza, for while. Carl looks at people and reads in the travel book, Jack makes some pictures and walking around, looking at the building, he is looking just like a pro photographer. The happy mode of Carl is coming to Jack to, making him

After a some minutes they walk into one of the side streets and finds a pizza restaurant, and gets an empty table and order, matter of course pizza, Italian style pizza, made in a stone own and some red wine. Soul of Italy is back, and they are really enjoying life. Jack tells Carl about the dream and why he likes the Dumbo, more than Duomo. He tells about that Maria and him have discussed a lot about angels, after that history, about Jesus and Mekka.

«That is a funny story, with some truth in it, replies Jack

«Yeah, I was sad about it for some time, but Maria, my angel, helped me out that one, and now I am here with my friend, in Italy, hunting of the truth.

«So, you mean that, the angel in that Cathedral is an evidence.

«Yes and no

«What do you mean, Jack asked with a big question face

«Life is a big puzzle, and sometimes collecting a lot of pieces makes a big picture.

«Yes, right about that, and a big picture has possibilities of many different fantasies.

«Yeah, maybe my Maria is an reincarnation of Maria Magdalena, and my Maria, it much more pretty than Maria Magdalena.

Jack laughs

«Your story reminds me of a trip I had to Paris. Do you want to hear it, is about bad things, going into nice things.

«yes, I want to learn everything in this world, and maybe telling them to others in my books.

«You are not a book writer yet, so stay grounded, my friend. The story was that I planed and went to Paris, I was going to visit a friend and look at Eiffel tower, Louvre, the art exhibition, some other attractions, and relax at some cafés. I went, happy away and got into a nice hotel, and after some hours of relaxing at a pillow, I went to the Eiffel tower, that thing is just like everybody must look at. When I got there, I got really disappointed. Bridges around the world is much more nice and complex built than that one, I thought, if that is the soul of Paris, then this country has trouble, because there are no soul in dead metal. After some photos, I went to a restaurants, got some nice food and perfect glass of red wine, there was a lot more soul of France, in that glass than in everything I had seen, that day. Later on I called my friend and we agreed, that he was going to pick me up at the hotel. We had been in contact via Internet threw an art forum, the thing I forgot, is that I don't know French. So we had a lot of communication problems, when I was at Internet, he wrote American, but now I was a guest, and his friends didn't know how to speak American, so I just felt like an Alien. I felt really sad, and went back to the hotel, then I meet some people from Netherlands, they spoke English, and my day was saved.

«Nice story, let us propose a toast of the soul of the soul of the healthiness in the red grapes.

«There is more in this story, bad thing going to happy things, want to hear more.

«Yes, I got plenty of time to a nice friendship, happy to know you in a different way than back at home.

«Agree to that one. Well, the next day I went to the Louvre to watch Mona Lise, that is an must, but she was on a vacation, aboard somewhere. I went looking at other pictures, they was really nice, but most of the signs telling the title of the pictures was in French. The happy of come of that day was that there was a Egyptian exhibition, and there I didn't have to read the French, because I just could read the signs, the hieroglyphs. They are pictures and telling their own stories. Later that day, I was thinking about what to do the next days, so I went buying a book, and a know I wanted to look at another museum, with pictures of Monet, Gauguin and so on. The point was that I really had forgot Picasso, he is a really funny artist. So next day, I went to Picasso museum, and learned a lot about him, I didn't know that he had made sculptures and theater costumes. He was brilliant with colors, and had the knowledge of that humans, have different masks, like we have, now I am at a vacation, when I am at work, I have different role. We are like actors everybody.

«So the conclusion is that Paris is a city with colorful French Fries.

«And a lot of churches, they got a cathedral to, heard about the Notre Dame, amazing, lot the movie, but I assume you not have seen that Disney movie, since you not got kids.

«Nope, but lets go back into our vacation city. Milan and have some more wine, there are a lot of soul in this one to.

«I think we have got enough red wine, lets walk back to the hotel and relax, this day is hot.

«I am happy to have an organizer with me, here is the route back to the hotel.

Jack picks up the map, and show a different route, than they walked this morning. First through the famous shopping marked and then along with some streets and a park, more streets and a piazza, turn right at piazza, and there the hotel is.

As they walk along the streets, they are looking around, looking at the people that passed by and the the buildings. As they are walking into the famous and historical shopping center side by side the Duomo, Carl replies.

«Hey, jack, look at that shop, he stops and turns around away from the shopping center

«Where are you going?

«I am not going into that stupid shopping center, I have found my second love in life, and he heads around the corner.

«What?

«The wild horse shop, real Italian red wild horses, The Ferrari shop

«I see, that building, that shopping center can wait, we are going to heaven

Like to small boys, they are heading to the shop, with big eyes. True beautifulness is heading into their mind. The walks into the shop and is looking around with big smiles.

«Carl, look at this design, I like this read one, and points to a red car.

«Me too, but this black one, is also nice, if I am going to sell a lot of books, I am going to buy one.

«Maybe, but you not no car today, but men are allowed to have toys.

«You should have one, Jack!

«I am a more family car type, shopping and kids...you will know one day, when you grow up, or maybe if you grow up.

«That is OK, but this one is magic

«Look at the these number at the engine, amazing

«vroooom, highway, is a flyway, going to the moon, very soon

Jack look at him and laughs

The trip to the shopping center is left to another day, while the memories of the cars are in their minds. They are looking around, not buying anything, and then the trip goes back to the start of the day, to the hotel, for a rest, the travel is still in the body, vacation can be hard too they agree. They are planning a dinner later in the evening, in the local area, nearby the hotel.

Eating and drinking is when we are feeding

Which resources needed which are counted

And we are able to share with a little fare

True love

That we will show

Later in the evening, they find a regular, pizzeria, if there is called something that is regular, anyway they are ordering salad, pizza, lot of water and a glass of red wine, make some small talking. When the pizzas arrive, the smell of fresh baked, is filling the room, and the cheese that is covering the top, is boiling, with a smell like true cheese, of the soul of the cow that has been walking in the green fields, in the mountains nearby. Fresh fields with, green grass. The bottom is thin, so the taste of the tomato sauce, that has been boiling for several hours, makes the taste excellent, quality food, made with a touch of feelings, that a chef puts into his cooking, to make the meal a tasty enjoyment, in harmony with the surroundings of the pizzeria. They are enjoying the meal in silence, and after the waiter, has cleaned up, Carl says.

«Jack, I have been thinking about something, about Paris.

«Great, you have been thinking, before you ask, progress. Just in a happy mode, what it my friend.

«You have been traveling a lot in Europe and seen a lot of famous pictures, do you ever see something magic about pictures, like signs ?

«Yes, in fact, I forgot to tell you about the think in Paris, in Louvre.

«What is that, Carl asks and is very interested

«I told you that Mona Lisa was gone in vacation, so I went into the bookstore at the museum, and there I got a book about the painting, a new book, and it claims that there are something about, the layer behind Mona Lisa, and that is very true, because there is something about mountains, red river and nature that is not so nice, as the portrait of the women.

«Very interesting, can I write it down

«Shore, but you got nothing to write on

«Look at the table, Carl smiles, here is a lot of paper

Jack laughs, and Carl gets a pen out of his pocket, and write some words, head words

«Ready for more, asks Jack

«Right on to the target.

«I have wondered a lot about that, because Leonardo da Vinci was a very clever man, and clever man like that is not making just some fantasy things, he constructed a lot of machines and studied the human body, he calculated that the ultimate number of the human body is 1618. You know that famous, drawing about the human body.

«I know about that, man standing in a circle. That is just a picture and ideal human, nobody is perfect. I have heard that 1618 is middle of earth, Mekka. I am not good with numbers, so I am not able the calculate that, maybe we can ask our strange friend, when we get home.

«Yes, we can do that. Interesting, because, further on writer claims that composition of the painting is very complex. Leonardo da Vinci was a very clever man, and the composition seems to be made of a pyramidal figure. So my suggestion is that he is telling us that mother earth is hurting, or going to be hurt if we don't change.

«Maybe that is right, this was very new to me and heavy stuff. Can you get the bill, and I will step outside to get a cigarillo, before we return to the hotel.

«Yes, I will do that.

Carl gets the big paper cloth and steps outside, the waiters that works in the restaurant, smiles and point their hands to the paper. Carl just puts his shoulders up, just like telling them, just life, use what you got in front of you.

Jack and Carl walks back to the hotel and are continuity talking. Maybe the wine have made the loosing up a little bit, and talking more, that they do at every days, one of the positive effects of the wine, making people, relax, get stress out of their bodies and just follow the wind, the vibrations of the atmosphere.

«So what is the plan for tomorrow, Carl.

«I feel something strange about walking with this cloth, so I need to get a writing book.

«Welcome to the new world, Carl, the new world is digital, why don't you get one of these small computers, mini PC.

«Thanks, my organizer, let go shopping tomorrow and maybe we can have a visit at your friend Leonardo da Vinci, the is an exhibition here, I have read on a poster, in the city center.

«Lets do that, I need some skirts too, so maybe we can drop into some shops to.

«We have that home too, shops

«We are in fashion Mekka. Think about that, when I step into the office with some new skirts, if comment about that, I am going to tell them, I just dropped into Milan this summer and bought some latest fashion. Ladies at work are going to be very impressed.

«Didn't know that you where up to flirting, with them.

«Just for fun, and it is more like I am telling them nice things and they are telling me nice things, not everything has to be focus on relationships, everybody needs some attention, in some way. Sharing positive thoughts, and energy.

«Aloha, my master, Jack, good night, see you tomorrow, Nine sharp?

«Night, nine sharp, to the tasty breakfast table, I am learning, of your positive energy.

They are back at the hotel and is turning back to their hotels rooms, while to moon rises the night, putting them into the state of dream sight.

Clothes are what we are wearing
Making us in a nice bearing
To keep us warm and calm
And keep us confident
And pleasant

Buying and selling
is not like betting
When we trade goods and favors
not like bookers
To satisfy our souls
Making us wholes

Crime and punishment is when
we talk like holy men
We act unfaithfully to our soul
Because we not are whole
In jealousy and misunderstanding
We use a bad branding

Hunting of treasures in fashion land

Jack is entering the breakfast room the next morning, some minutes past nine. Carl is sitting at a table, with a a cup of espresso in from of him and waiting something to happen. He is reading a newspaper.

«God morning, what is in the news ?

«I don't know, but it seems that they are interested in the same thing that we are home. Writing about what is happening, criticizing each other, telling about accidents, regular stuff.

«I am so lucky to be free of that world, now I am ready to be in the fantasy world, but first I need some coffee. Jack turns around, before getting down at the table, and makes a sign to the waitress.

She looks at him and walks to the table.

«Bon journo

«Espresso, please, large

She smiles, and tells him "grazie"

Carl starts to laugh

«What?, replies Jack

«New day, new world, I can see

«Just learning, from a nice friend and use my new knowledge of how to live in this world. Still feel a little bit strange in this country, it is like being a part of a movie.

«I know, my first travels was like that to

«Well, lets get a lot of this food so we are ready to enter the world of shopping

«Yes

«Going from shop to shop, wondering what we are going to have

«Hey, I am not a woman

«Just kidding, buddy, that is the nice about staying here with a friend, we are just right on the target. We got a mission, not trying to put the whole fashion world together, like does is fit. It is quite funny to look at, how the world looks like, the shopping world. Do you know what one of the greatest philosophers said, when he visit a marked of the first time in his life, in Athens.

«No

«I am very happy to see all the things I don't need. I am a happy guy.

«But he needed to have something

«He was just carrying a book, a book to write about his knowledge

«But that was some thousand of years ago

«You are right, the world is becoming easier, we don't want to live like that. We have not been able to enjoy, this sugar, with come color, and a shot of caffeine.

«Well stay grounded, and finish your food, things to do.

«Yes, right on, my mouth is empty with words.

They finish up with the breakfast and return to their rooms, to get ready to their exploration trip in shopping land, streets of fashion. Maybe it is not their passion, but inside somewhere they like to buy things, new things, making their hearts sings, even if it is technique, anyhow if words that heat their cheeks and having blank eyes, that is telling lies.

They get into the streets and are walking down, towards the city center. This they is hot to, but not so hot as the days before. They stops at some windows to watch what they have got. After a some stops, Carl heads into a shop, walking strait into some skirts. Looking at them, picks two and them, and walks to a woman, that is working there and asks if she think that is the right size. She is looking at him with eyes, that is measuring his body, and she agrees. He is walking into the test room, stays for some minutes and walks out again, putting the skirts beside the cash machine and get his wallet out of the pocket and pulls out his credit card to pay. Jack is just standing, and watching, he has got a little smile on his face and have some thoughts about whats happened. Carl returns ho him and says

«I got my things, lets go ahead and get your things

«Your shopping act was, funny

«Funny?

«Yes, you had the look of just you knew what where you wanted, it was just like you had the pictures in your head and went, just to get what fit you images in your head.

«Maybe you are right about that one, not bad Jack, not bad

«Before I left, I have been talking and reading about colors, colors of people. Lets talk more about that later.

«You are amazing me, Jack

«Just investigating, or research is the right word. Lets speed up, and get my things, before someone else is getting my stuff.

«Big possibilities of that

«In a kind of way, you are acting strange today

«What ?

«Is nothing, just my mind, that forgot to tell me shut up Jack.

«What ever.

They are turning out in the street of shopping again, a new task is set, they are walking around, to get some shops that sell electronic stuff, but it is not so easy to find in this shopping area. They are not giving up, so they walks around. They find some shops that is selling these kind of stuff, and they steps inside, most of the employees are not talking American, so they are using hands and fingers to tell what they are looking for. Some places are sold out and some just have a demo, a empty plastic model, so they can order.

Near by the cathedral there is a large shop have a lot of goods, in many different categories, and Jack is heading straight to a glass show case with several small computers. He smiles, just like kid, finally found his favor toy in the whole world, that is what he just wants. He walks to the counter, and talks to the man that is behind. The man speaks American, and is just about to tell him about the machine, but Jack just stops him and tells him that he is buying one right now and picks up a credit card, from his pocket. The man looks a bit strange, but is happy to have a customer to know what he wants, it is his profit to. The man tells him that he got several in the storage room, and walks away to get one.

While they are waiting, there are several customers looking at some mobile phones, they are looking, and wondering what they are going to buy, or maybe they are just looking and going to buy another day.. There are several types, from many vendors, some of them look almost alike, just a different brand. Maybe the functions are the same too.

The counter man is returning from the storage room, and makes the papers ready. Jack is picking up the machine and the parts that belongs to the machine, tells the man that he is going to use it right away, and puts the wrapping into a dustbin that is behind the desk. People are stirring at Jack, and he smiles back at them, and telling them with his body language, I got what I wanted and that makes me very happy. Jack returns to Carl, with his smiling body. Carl have been looking at some films in another part of the store.

«Mission completed, but I need a carry case

«Right, replies Carl

«Lets walk into some of the side streets, maybe they got something

«That seems to be a good idea

«Are you going to buy anything, at this store, or are you ready to leave the store.

«Lets leave, American films, with Italian text or dubbing is not on my wish list.

«You are in a funny mood today

«Maybe I got a funny friend, that makes me happy.

«Thanks, let continue our hunting of treasures, in fashion land

They are walking out of the store and are heading to some stores that have bags. Hunting a bad seems to be lot easier, than getting the mini PC, and Jack is picking a backpack, so it is easy to carry. The hunt of physical objects of the day is finished, and they are looking around to get a nice quite place to get some lunch. After a couple of tries they are getting a small table at a sandwich bar, nearby.

«This really need a celebration, I am having a glass of wine, and some of what you are eating, going to order, thing. Says Jack with a big smile.

«I guess that is a an tuna sandwich, and a glass of white wine.

«Tasty, this is a nice day, I really like Italy

«Agree to that, Jack

Carl tries to make a sign to the waiter, that passes the table, but he is just heading strait to another table.

«Not my table, replies Jack, whispering to Carl. Rules of the world. One of the international rule that everyone has to respects.

«Copy that, Jack

«Here is our table master coming, the right one

Carl makes the order, and the waiter replies with an American accent that is more like African. He smiles, and put the order to his notebook, and returns to the kitchen.

«He really seems to be nice, he was really polite, look at the other waiter, it seems that he is flirting with the customer.

Carl looks in the direction of the waiter and comments

«Yes, you are right, and they are both men

«Maybe the customer is paying for extra service

«Be careful now, I just think we are going to talk about that, they chose their own lives

«I was more thinking about, if this was my business, I would be angry at that waiter, because he is using private time and my business. He has no respect of the owner of this place. The reputation of this place can be bad, and that will make them bankrupt.

«Calm down, you left that job, enjoy the sandwich and the wine.

«You are right, thanks

«Let us finish up and walk to the Leonardo da Vinci exhibition.

«Lets do that, your telling about Mona Lisa made my interested, maybe we can discover something new, like trying to get into his mind, what did he think.

«With your fantasy, this is going to very interesting.

«Maybe it is just not fantasy, maybe there are something about the facts of to

«That is right, and you make these facts into funny stories. I just think you are going to be a nice writer

«Tanks, that reminds me about that I need some power to my new PC. I am stepping inside, to get some power and recharge this thing, so I can start to write right away.

«I just think, that can wait, let us pay and go away on exploration.

They finish up the lunch and are walks away into the exhibition, that is just some minutes away. They are getting some tickets and entering the show. Jack and Carl walks to a sign in the start of the exhibition, and it says, what they are about to see, the are some of the drawings of the artist. Jack stops along with the reading of the open. Carl walks to a touch screen, that has a system where they can navigate, from one drawing to another drawing, with just a gentle touch of a finger. There are several other visitors there, and they all are looking with interest of the drawing

«It was amazing that he was able to make all these inventions, he made constructions of things that was build several hundred of years later, like the airplane.

«Yes, he is amazing, still wondering about, the story you told me, about the painting of Mona Lisa. I think you are right, he was to clever to just make a picture of fun. He has got an extroverted mind, and I am very happy to learn from him

«Didn't you read the sign

«What sign ?

«The text he wrote

«No

«Go back and look

«I will do

Jack goes back and reads the text. He reads it, again and again. Suddenly he almost freeze like and statue. Carl is looking at him and walks towards him, with a big smile.

«So Jack, got his message

«Yes, I got it, the meaning of don't learn this boy

«BE CREATIVE, they both is telling each other, as they laughs together.

«And you my friend, is doing that it with a smile, in a fantasy mind

Laws is rules we use to
use our IQ
Put our souls into respect
in a nice aspect
to other humans
without any burdens

«Let go outside and make a break, from this science world

«I am going to stay here for some more minutes, replied Jack

«Ok, I will just get a book at the bookstore next door, so long, see you outside, at the statue, with the great man, and his four disciples.

Carl walk out of the building, and into the bookstore. There are a lot of art books. He stops just inside the store, and looks around. Just thinking what to get. After some seconds, he gets an idea. He walks around and finds a shelf about Leonardo da Vinci. He looks threw the books and finds a large book, with the painting of Mona Lisa at the front cover, he walks happy to the counter desk, and gets some Euro bills out of his pocket, and pays. Then he walk outside, and finds an open sitting place in the shadow, of the sculpture. He starters to turn over the pages and reads some, but doesn't find anything interesting. He starts to look at the painting with big interest, just like that he wants to find something that nobody has discovered yet. He turns the book up side down, puts from the book as long that his arms reaches, the he gets a smile. I got the code.

Jack is coming out of the exhibition, with a DVD in his hand. Looking quite happy. He walks towards Jack, that is laughing quietly and is in his own world. He steps up to him and says

«What ?

«I have discovered the code

«The code ?

«Yes, you got it wrong, you are to serious, and the man that analyze the painting, as you described.

«Well, tell me your theory

«The painting is about the beautifulness of the women, the soul of a woman

«What

«Have to heard of the poem, beauty of the woman

«No

«I am going to tell you, it is a very secret, the man who understands that poem, and tells it to a woman, got a really big ace one his hand.

«That is new to me, tell me

He tells about it, and explains about the eyes and the soul. The magic in the eyes and the soul is like understanding each other. He further explains that he has not understood the ending, the part telling about, passion, until now. In ancient Egypt they use the sign of an eye quit often, as a symbol of Horus eye, Yin and Yang connection, Soul mates find it to see themselves in that lifetime with you.

«Passion is how to complete a two souls, man and woman, soul mates. Passion is about how to satisfy each other. Women like sex too.

«I know that

«You see, the painting is about, the soul of a woman, the river is the blood, like the soul. Mountains is like bad and good days, eyes is like talking to each other, communication. He had the ability to see the women, in a different way. As you have told me about paintings, it is both about getting inside and outside of the model. See the real person, not only the pretty face.

«Still don't know what the link is ?

«The idea, or the theory, as you told me, I just got under this statue. The statue tells me that he has four helpers, working with him. And one of them is a poet, and that is not something we know about, but maybe the poet was a writer and a poet. Leonardo came to Milan, and finished the painting, before he was moved to Rome. Italy was divided into two parts, north and south, that is why he didn't make more paintings.

«I just got of the track, Carl

«The idea of the poem, came to me when I looked up at that poet

«I am still not with you

«Forget the last part, and the painting is about as you explained, about triangles

«Yes

«If you turn the painting, just up side down. What do you see ?

Carl gives the book to Jack, and turns it upside down. Jack looks at it for a long time, but still doesn't get it. He is a big question in his face.

«What ?

«Carl points at the triangle

«What ?

«How where you born

«Just like others, of my mother

«Yes, and where did you come out, and how did you got make

«Aaah, come on, you are just homesick. Keep your fantasy in you own mind, about that one.

«Just a theory

«Just a fantasy

«I just like this story, better than the other one. Who is in the mind of that man, nobody.

«It is funny story, that I will remember about for a long time

They both smiles, for a long time and gets up and starts to walk against to hotel. The day is hot, so they need a long siesta, to get away from the sun and the heat. The heat is making the air above the ground just like a mirage, or look like the road turns into diffuse mirage. Just after couple of minutes, the get into a cab and finds it very pleasant to get into a car with air condition. They are not talking much, but when they get back to the hotel, they agree a time to meet in the evening, to get dinner, somewhere around the hotel.

Later in the evening, they meet in the lobby, and they are ready to go. Carl have with him, his new electronic wonder under his arm.

«So you got a new friend, says Jack and points at the machine

«It was just a little unpractical to write one the cloth

«Yes, but I will remember it, it was a nice tip, maybe I can use it in work.

«Yes, well I did, so why not

«Lets walk

«I was thinking, why do we not do something different today, go somewhere else

«Nice, any suggestions

«Lets get a cab, and go back to city center, maybe we can go into the famous shopping center by the Duomo.

«OK

They order a taxi at the lobby, and the cab, arrives in couple of minutes. Carl tells the driver, to take them to the city center.

The taxi is stopping outside the statue of Leonard da Vinci and they walk into the shopping center, after the payment is done.

«Where do you want to go ?

«I would like a nice place, doesn't have to be the most expensive, but somewhere that is some quality.

«that is fair, because I don't can afford to be at a expensive place because writers doesn't seems to have much money.

«But I think that writing will give you more pleasure, that thinking about money, if you think and write with your heart.

«Write with my heart, I am going to write with my fingertips, running these key like the wind.

«but you got something to write about

«Maybe I can write about, secret signs, like those you are telling me about in that painting.

«That is symbolic expression, of an painter

«Do you have any other suggestions

«What about to start with poems

«I don't know how to do that, but I discovered people, how they look, they are different in colors

«How?

«They dress like colors, of astronomy

«Do they ?

«Yes, they do, Maria tipped me about that ?

«How does I look like then ?

«You look like black, dressed for style, women looks at you

«Maybe that, I don't know

«How are you then ?

«I am maybe more dressing like a lion

«How ?

«I don't really don't know, but Maria tells me that I look like an, and act like that

«Are you borne lion ?

«No

«Interesting, maybe you can learn me, maybe we can discover something together, in paintings

«Yes, but I am not shore of that painters does know that, because that is an observation of humans

«How ?

«Look at the people that is sitting across the other side

«Yes

«Look at the women, how they dress, colors

«Yes, they dress different

«What color do you like best ?

«I don't know, maybe white, but that is different from day to day, when I am here, I dress different than at work. What color do you like then ?

«Maybe blue and green

«Conservative ?

«No, more like creative and communicative

«hmm, strange

«When we get home, I guess you will see it more easy, because it is hot these days, so maybe the colors are not shown correctly, but you know that woman have a lot of tops.

«That is for shore

«When they buy these tops, choice of color is not accidental, they are projecting they DNA, or they personality in they colors.

«Maybe that

«Look across at those Muslim womens, they got different colors at their heads.

«Yes, you are right about that.

«One of the things I studied back at home before I left was these colors.

«Interesting

«Let get some food and go to another place later, for some coffee and maybe a brandy.

«Nice, but I think grappa is the thing down here.

«What is that ?

«Something liquor, made of grapes, but in Italian way, sometimes nice, sometimes horrible.

They make a short dinner, they do some small talking, enjoying the taste and aesthetic look of the the food. Carl is happy of that jack made him going to this place, it kind of serves them a different taste of the food. The look, the smell and their surroundings, the people looks like different, they are colored, telling personalties, whom they really are. Jack sees not that people are different, and he is very happy to learned these colors of humans. Some people says that alchemy is strong in the north part of Italy, moved away from the

Cristian surrounding, that is around Rome and going south to the tip of the shoe, the tip that looks like that is it kicking Cicily, far away out of the Mediterranean sea, more like that is it going to land into the Atlantic ocean.

They walk away slowly after the dinner, they agree that they need some fresh air. Carl asked where to go, where is the hottest place in they city, where does all the hot shots go in this city. He writes up the name of the place at the backside of the receipt.

«Let us walk to that place, we need some exercise, and the temperature is making it into a pleasure.

One of the nice thing about walking is that we can do windows shopping, look at what they got, without having anything to buy, and the lights in the windows are made to let them look nice in the evenings, maybe like a invitation, this is what we got, our designs. Milan is latest fashion, thing that is going to arrive later in other countries. Jack really likes the suites, with a modern design, dark ones with small details that make them something magic, a little touch of a designer hand, that has made into that label it is connected to.

«It seems to be upcoming some bad weather

«Maybe, but this is like normal in the Mediterranean sea. Especially by the alps

«How ?

«The sun heats the sea at these days, and clouds are trying to reach the tops of this mountains, that is why it is so green here, not in Milan, but a little bit closer to the mountain.

«I get what you are talking about.

Far away they are able to see some flashes, that lighten ups the marvelous mountain, that is in front of them, in the north, they are not able to see them, but the flashes in the dark clouds, tell them where they are.

They walks along with the streets, streets with marble buildings. One of the magic things about Italy. They arrive into their destination, the are several pillars holding the facade of the front part, making is more exclusive look. There are tables with a garden look in front, brown ones with white pads. Between there are green small hedges, and glass tables with candle lights, making it a little bit romantic. There are sitting people at most of these tables, but the is a empty space in the middle, it seems that nobody wants to be in the middle of the attraction. Jack and Carl don't care, and they enjoy to sit in the middle, so they can look at what is happening. A waiter is coming towards them.

«Coffee and Grappa, says Carl with a firm and gentle voice

«What kind, says the waiter

«Just make, something that you think suits me, this is the first time

«Gin & Tonic, and a espresso, says Jack

The waiter turns around, and enters into the building, the place smalls style, men got suites and women got dresses.

«What about a color game

«Lets do that

«I see that you have got a lot of attention already, they are looking at you, so don't look to much if you don't have any intention of learning Italian very fast

«I get it, I am used to it, Jack replies

«Look at that table, where there are several women, and only one man. What do you see ?

«Colors ?

«Yes

Jack carefully looks at them, without staring. More like just moving his eyes, and holding his head in position. Observing the colors.

«He turns, back they are just different, all of them.

«Not like, but she in black is nice

«Maybe you find her like a friend.

«Maybe

«She looks at you, and is telling somethings with her eyes, friendship and understanding.

«Your right about that one.

«She in pink, looks at you in interesting mode, Carl laughs

«Yeah, lets finish up, and get back, playing games in not my thoughts

«Let us relax some minutes, enjoy the atmosphere, look stars are coming.

«Nice

They are both looking into the sky, and a lot of stars are covering they black background, that covers the universe.

«We are not going to stay for long, tomorrow is our last they, before traveling along.

I want to watch the DVD of the drawing, maybe I can borrow your machine, if you are not going to use it yourself.

«Not tonight, I am tired

«Nice, lets get a taxi

They get a taxi and return to the hotel, and their rooms, making a good night sleep, ready to do more exploring the day after.

Freedom is when we are true

To know what to do

To our souls in love of life

into the wildlife

Sunday walk in Milan

The agreed the evening before, that they would meet after breakfast. It is Sunday, so a relaxing day is in front of them. Shops and traffic is slowing down. Stress that the inhabitants of this city.

«Good morning

«Good morning

«Ready of a slow day

«Yes

«Lets go to the park, and then to the Borgia

«Castle is a better word

«Thanks, you are in a understandable mode

«Yes

«I am ready, are you ?

«Park is going to be nice, a change of these street, lets walk

They are walking out to the street. The street that leads to the park. The entrance of the park is nice, looking like a portal, and makes a nice separation from the city life into a green world. There are several families in the park. small families, and larger families. They are walking and just enjoying the park. They stops at a bench an opposite barrel organ. A man is singing, with nice voice, more like a tenor, his wife is selling balloons to the children. It seems that they are doing it to make the visitors happy, and not for the money. He sings in Italian, and they enjoy the singing. He is not a super star, but makes them in Italian mode. They listens to a couple of songs and walks away, after putting some coins into a hat, that is in front of the singer, a sign of that have had an enjoyable time.

«It seems that Italian families is just like home, Jack says

«Maybe

«Have though about getting children

«My life have been, strange, maybe busy

«So, you have though about it

«Yes, Maria have asked

«And ?

«I have told her, that I am not ready

«Is she ?

«I guess, so but timing to both of us is bad

«Maybe

«You got a child

«Yes, and she is lovely, making my life great

«Maybe I can join you, when we get back, so I can learn.

«That is nice, I will tell you next time I got her at my home, says Jack

«Great

«I think that you can be a great dad, you are funny and good about talking in feelings, I am learning from you.

«Thanks, Jack, and he smiles

They are walking along with the park. The park is covered with large trees a lot of flowers in many different colors, and some small playgrounds to the children. They stops in front of some people, that is performing some kind of yoga. Jack stops first, and Carl follows.

«I think they are amazing, replies Jack

«Yes

«Look, there is a old man to

«Shore

«Not your kind of training

«No

«I am going to, make an course this autumn

«Really?

«Yes, I have heard that is better than running, in Asia they do a lot of it and they are very healthy. Slim.

«Well, you can join them, just go ahead.

«No

«Come on

«But I am going to join that course, but that is in the autumn

Carl laughs and say to him

«You are little bit afraid

«Maybe

«I understand that, because it is different, that what you are used to.

«You are right, lets walk away, to the castle

They walk out the gate, and in the direction of the castle. They are looking at the buildings, and

After some minutes, there are looking at a woman coming towards them. She has a typical model look, a high fashion look. Carl stops, steps a side to make her a clear walk and Jack follows. Jack is looking at Carl, Carl is looking at the model with a wondering look.

«She almost look sick, Carl says with a quite voice, when she has passed them.

«Yes, the fashion world are though to them.

«Yes, but they look good in magazines, but she looked sick

«Pictures are lying

«What ? How ?

«First, it looks often that pictures are adding some pounds, So at a picture she looks different.

«ohh

«The world has become digital, so changing a picture is quite easy. Like is the model has a bad day, dark lines under her eyes, they can fix it.

«Yes, I have heard that, I seen it lot of times in the finance magazines. The look like kings and queens at the picture, and are looking quite different at work. These are hard working people.

«Models work very hard to. A photo sessions takes hours

«Maybe that is true, I don't know, but now I know

«You are welcome

«How do you know these things

«Well, you know that I take photos and is interested in art

«Yes

«To be a better photographer myself, I have looked at a lot of photos, trying to understand how the photographer thinks.

«I don't see the link to the art, art and photos are different

«I will say, yes and no

«How ?

«To understand a picture, what the painter is trying to tell, you have to have to understand the picture. A picture can be telling a whole story.

«Yes, Carl says with a big smile and laughs

«So you are still thinking about Mona Lisa

«Yes, and I am going to figure out what he really though, that man didn't paint that picture just for fun.

«Maybe for money

«Maybe, but the story you told me, is telling me more

«You are going to winder about that picture for several days

«Maybe you are right about that, but I am going to make up something.

«Well, write it don't one day

«i want to discuss it with you, you seems to have quite good understanding.

«I know something, but I am not an expert.

«Expert are no fun, that is like going to a study, teachers don't use to be fun

«You are right about that, but there are some.

«Yes, but on the other side, if the teacher was just a joke, would the students believed him

«Or her

«Equality sex fantasy man! Rise you flag

«Come one, welcome to the world

«I just think that we are going to drop that one

«Right, lets go into that museum, as a break on out Sunday trip

«I am following you, my friend

They are walking into a museum. Jack asks what it is and get an explanation that it is a gallery, and a museum, with old pictures. Jack pays the tickets and they are walking up the marble stairs that leads them up to the first floor. Carl stops, between to floors, and is looking up in to celling. He looks a couple of seconds, and says

«Stairway to heaven, with a big smile

«What ?

«Angles, lots of them, heaven

Jack laughs and replies

«This is going to be the most interesting gallery exhibition in my life, you fun words and your fantasy is making me wondering about that I am entering into a new world that I never have seen before.

«Hey, you told me, to be inside the artist, so that is what his thought where. This is heavens look. Lets walk into the gallery, so Mr. Expert can tell me what to look at.

Jack, smiles and they are walking up to the first floor. They start to walk to the left, there are three rooms separated with door cases. Jack walks around and is looking, Carl follows him, and watches him. He is trying to look at what Jack is watching. Jack stops a long time in front of a picture.

«So what do think about that one, says Carl

«I think the painter has done a great job. Quality is great, a lot of fine hand work.

«Maybe the painter admired that priest a lot. So that is why this painting is so great.

«Paintings are like photos back at that time.

«Yes, I know that, just kidding

«Ohh, I was in the painting, and forgot that I have a funny friend with me.

«Maybe that man was a great man, a man with many words, a nice preacher.

«Rich people where able to get them painted, back at that at old times

«Yes, and the men of church was a lot of money back at the old days

«Men of knowledge

They are walking around. Looking more at the pictures. In the end of the gallery, there is a room to the left with old watches. This is a exhibition of the oldest clocks in Milan. They are looking abound, and Carl is watching a clock for a long time. Jack walks up to him and says

«What ?

«This one is very old, almost before that the church told us to follow the time, and organization of the world.

«What ? Jack says and is looking at Carl to understand if this is a joke or if it is real.

«Well, a pope decided, that the whole Christian world, needs rules, how to organize people, so he told that watches is how we are going to live.

«Clocks are nice, replies Jack

«Yes, but the world doesn't need to follow it. Walk back, do you think that the painters like clocks.

«It is a helpful tool

«That is right, you should add, it is a helpful tool and not a living rule

Jack, smiles to him.

«What ?

«Nothing

«Sometimes you hide information from me

«Just an observation, Jack says and is walking away. Carl is looking around more and is really looking close to these clocks. Jack walks out to the main room, where they started and Carl catches up with him some minutes later.

«Are you finished, asks Jack, when Carl returns

«Not yet, can you make my a photo of that picture ?

«I think that is not possible, because the is not enough light, the picture is going to be dim.

«Can you try ?

«Well, seems to be important to you, so I will try

Jack, makes some photos, he shake his head and shows them to Carl.

«That is great, I just don't more than that

«What is it about

«I am going to tell you later, I need lunch, lets us leave heaven and enter the streets again

«Good idea, jack says with a smile

They step outside of the gallery and continue to walk in the direction of the castle. A nice small café is in sight and they find themselves a table. They sit quite, looking at the piazza where the café is. It in front of a small snack bar, old one, with green doors, the tables are surrounded with a small fence, and as most piazza are like, there is a church. Carl looks at the people, and starts to look at a young couple that is sitting across to his table. He looks at them some minutes, and turn away when the young woman is looking in his direction. The food is arriving their table and Jack asks.

«You turned so strange some minutes ago

«Ohh, you know the idea of the colors.

«What ?

«Well I did not believe in the start, but the more I look at people, this is the truth, Maria was right.

«You are strange, but you look so serious, like that you are performing a research.

«Yes, that is true

«Well, that is above my knowledge, and I think that you need more facts, this is just something that you see.

«Yes, but it is a prof of that science is true.

«Astrology is not science

«Well, if you see in history books, there is a lot writings about it.

«And ?

«I just got a new prof today at that galley

«What ?

«Someone changed the truth

«What ?

«You know that picture you made that photo

«Yes

«Did you see what is was ?

«As I remember, it was Maria and Jesus, with a bible.

«The truth, and learning of you, about painters, how they think

«Yes

«Maria was telling a story, a fairy tail, Jesus, was painted with a youngster face together with a baby body. He was pointing into the book.

«I don't get the point

«There are some talking about that the bible is changed in the history, that the true words was hidden. Knowledge was great power back at these old times.

«I don't know, Jack replies and pulls his shoulders upwards, and marks a questioning face.

«I realized, the truth inside that gallery, because it was like walking in history, change of times.

«How ?

«The paintings before 1600 was a lot about angels, Jesus and Maria, and then a pope in Rome decided to use the clock, and paintings changed.

«Maybe just a new era

«Yes, true, time of information

«Come on

«There is another thing to, about colors of the clothes

«What fantasy is that ?

«Red is a powerfull color and blue is communicative

«Maybe

«If you mix together red and bluem you get mauve or lilac, the color that priest uses, the higest ranked

«Paintings of clothes to Jesus is never lilac, the color is usually red and blue. He is telling somethings, not telling this is the truth. He gave the people a choice.

«Maybe

«What do you belive in then

«I don't know, mostly nice people, people that cares in a posetive way

«Agree about that, but if someone is not telling the truth, what then

«Maybe we not should beleive in them

«But I need to beleive in something

«We all do, maybe, seems that nothing can be at prof

«Guess so, lets eat and get on the road again

The day is hot, so they make a short lunch, and heads to the the castle with, thoughts of expectations of new experience. They get tickets and a map of the castle just to left side of the great gate to the castle that has been unchanged for hundred of years. In the middle of the castle there is a large space covered with walk paths and green grass. They start inside the castle. There is a exhibition up some stairs, first they look at some old music instruments. Carl I very fascinated of the them, the evolution in music has been great the last 500 years. They walk in silence. They continue to the end of the exhibition, and that room have a lot of carpets handing from the roof. Carl stops and looks at them, walks around, and is smiling more and more. He walks up to Jack, that has stopped at the exit.

«What do you think about them

«Nice, not my kind of art

«Yes, but the pictures in the carpets

«Didn't look at that

«Take a new look, what are these prophets pointing at

Jack walks to them and get a new look, there are several carpets, so he walks the whole round thew the room.

«Come on, says Jack, when he gets back

«What?

«Fantasy!

«Yes, shore, me and the artist is fantasizing about that these prophets are pointing to these astrological signs.

«I need a break, lets walk out of the castle and into the park, maybe I will get you on the ground

Carl laughs, and says «i am always at the ground, just look at my feet

«You are worse than lawyers. I am just going to buy a souvenir book and lets walk.

Carl laughs, and follows him like a soldier out the castle and into the park that is just outside the gate. The day is still hot and they pick with them some water, and heads to she shadow under a one of the first trees. This park is quite different, than the other they visit earlier this morning. There a lot of couples and groups with friend, some of them are have guitar and singing songs.

«Old familiar American songs, with Italian accent, says Carl

«Yes, nice to get out of your fantasy world, you are making me crazy

«Hope not so, laughs Carl

«Well you have made art into a new thinking to me

«How ?

«That it is very easy to make a story about a picture and a long story if you make them together

«Maybe that, I just want to have some fun

«That is nice

«Can you hear that drums ?

«Yes

«They are nice, making this park alive. Join me!

Carl gets up at his feet, and is walking in the direction of the drums. It is an African sound, djembe drums, thats make the typical African sound. Jack seems to have no choice so he just follow on. They walk a couple of minutes, and finds them a nice place in front of the drummers. There are several, some of them have Italian look, some have not. They are siting in a circle, made like a tribune, with three levels. It seems that one of them is the leader, and other follows. They sit quietly and listens to the music, in four melodies. Jack reads his new book and Carl follows the music.

«Didn't know that you like that kind of music, says Jack

«I just like all kind of music, happy music

«Do you know notes ?

«No, but I know tones, we had a piano back at home

«Do you know how to play ?

«Nope, but I tried just for fun, never got any education. I was the tough guy and still is.

«Yes, you are! Jack laughs

Carl follows the rhythm of the music, and Jack says

«Do you know what they are singing ?

«Nope, maybe

Pure love, pure love

As every humans show, a nice wind will flow

Hearts will forever glow

Pure love, pure love, free love free love

Peace and love, Peace and love

Jacks looks at Carl for a long time, with a very big smile and says

«You have a talent

«What ?

«Writing songs

«Ahh, come on, now you are making fantasies. Let us go to the city center for dinner, before the sunstroke kills you. Carl laughs

They walk out of the park, and Carl picks up his map, to get the direction. He uses a long time, to find the way back, and then he looks up and tells Jack.

«Ready for new exploration and travel of Milan

«What ? Says Jack, with some fear in his voice

«The tram, the yellow trams

«Seems to be nice

«Follow the leader

They walk to the tram stop, that is a couple of minutes walk away, they have to run the last yards to get into the tram that is waiting. Carl asks the driver how to pay, but the driver just pull up his shoulders, making a sign that he don't sell tickets. The driver gives them a sign to walk into the tram. They just walks along. He follows the map and when they reach city center, they pull the stop button and walks out, there are several other people getting off at the same stop. Outside, there are several inspectors, checking the tickets. They start to talk to Carl and Jack in Italian, but they don't understand, the guards don't understand American, but finally with a lot of pointing and some simple words, they got one penalty each and a smile from the inspector

«Our lucky day, says Carl

«Great leadership, says Jack and handle the penalty note to Carl

«Thanks, needed that one to, to make some great notes, Carl laughs

They are walking towards one of the most famous shopping streets in Milan to find somewhere, there are a lot of people. Traditional Italian music is in the air. They find them a nice restaurant, with a great view of the people passing by. They do they orders, and are sitting and waiting. Carl looks at the people passing by and Jack reads his book. Carl turns to Jack and says

«Hey, Jack

He looks up of his book and is ready to listen, and replies

«Yes

«Look across the street

«What

«That model has to be fed

«Hey, don't take take one, Carl, I think she is sick

«What?

«Maybe she has been a model, but got an image that she is fat, so her mind gets sick

«I got it, sorry, bad joke

«Yes, really

Jack puts his mind into his book and continues his study of the text and the pictures. Carl gets thoughtful.

«Hey, Jack

«Yes, with a little bit irritation in his voice of the distraction

«Got a pen?

«Yes, he says, I got one in your bag

Carl looks in his bag, and find the pen and some paper. He puts the paper at the table and makes an circle. Jack look at him and asks

«What are you up to?

«Just a master idea

«A master idea?

«Master of masters

Jack laughs, and says «Come on, show me, you got me

Carl looks at him with a big smile, and looks down to the paper and point at the circle

«This circle is Mr. Genius work, Leonardo da Vinci

«Yes ?

«This is the earth, Mona Lisa painting is the beauty of Gaia, earth is beautiful, mother earth.

Carl looks at Jack to see if he follows the idea, he recognize that, he doesn't understand, and says

«The background of Mona Lisa painting is a illustration Gaia, and the construct of the painting in Mona Lisa is the pyramids. He tells us this in the famous man picture to, the center of the world is at the pyramids in Cairo.

«I have seen that sign in the new age thinking. These two triangles. Maybe you are up to something.

«That is for shore!

«Have you got more?

«Yes, I realized that this today. The ancient Egyptian know that the earth was a globe. The knew that there was many planets, just like the Mayan people.

«Wow, explain

«There are a lot of hieroglyphs at the walls, both in Egyptian and Mayan buildings.

«Yes

«Leonardo da Vinci was very smart, if you look at the drawings of the castle, is also two pyramids. He made a lot of drawings about Atlantis, so maybe he knew in somehow, that it is hidden in the other side of the earth, a continent that was going down in the earth, because it was placed in a place with a lot of volcanoes.

«How?

«Continent's are moving, millions of years ago, Africa and America was together

«Yes?

«Maybe Atlantis is between, so Leonardo da Vinci, draw a lot of tools, to how to get there, into the deep.

«If that is true, you should work on that when we get back home, and write about it, but I still think this is a fantasy

«Maybe

«Anyway, I don't know, but write about it.

«Thanks, maybe I will do

«Nice, but first, we need a couple of days in Venice, to smell the ocean.

«Neptune, here we come

They finished up and walked back to their hotel, with making the last evening passing the windows of fashion, to make the memories of Milan into their minds.

Reason and passion is when we are
like a world star
True love in our souls
Having nice goals
To the earth and humans
Feeling like tall canyons

Pain is when our souls
Doesn't meet our goals
Is bad treaded in the way of
the true love
Jealously or misunderstanding
is like blaming
True love is free
That is what we want to be

Traveling Venice

Next morning, they rushed down to the train station, new experience was in front of them. A short breakfast was in their stomachs, and suitcases, was filled with new treasures. They was a little bit stressed, but at the arrive and the view of the marble train station, and tickets in their hands made them calm. Traveling of couple of hours threw the landscape of northern Italy was in their minds. This day was hot too, and the chilly feeling of the air condition in the train was a welcome pleasure to their bodies. Chairs separated with a small table, by the window, gives them a great view.

«This is going to be perfect

«Yes

«I kind of like nature

«How ?

«The touch a silence

«maybe, let us see, what the trip gives us

The train moved out of the station, passing houses of the city, houses changes from business buildings then to flats and the to suburbia houses before the they reach the open fields. The landscape to the south is covered of with rolling fields of wheat, separated by small towns made in Italians style. A church and some surrounding buildings made of bricks in colors of terracotta and red roofs. Some large wide green threes. Outside these small villages there are some farms with a castle looking buildings surrounded by wine grapes and roads up to these farms are covered with avenues of poplars.

To the north the mountains of the alps steep high into the write clouds, that look like cotton balls sticked to the tops. Small villages can be seen in the rise up to these mountains, these mountains that is covered with green hill fields.

Carl is looking out the window and starts to wave his head, slowly slowly

«What are you up to now ?

«I was just thinking about music, wondering how they write music, and I got an idea

«How ?

«Is you look at these rolling fields, and put music to them it is almost like poetry

«Or maybe the other way

«Good point, good point, my friend.

They are arriving Venice train station two hour later, after passing the sea that covers both sides of the last miles out to the city. The water is almost green and the sky is blue, making it into a fantastic view.

«So how are we going to the hotel when , when we get to Venice

«Well, I got a plan

«And that is

«We travel in action

Jack laughs and says «How?

«Well, first we grab our bags, then we run down to the canal, jump into a taxi boat, and tell the taxi driver to drive fast fast fast

Jack laughs again «What movie was that from ?

«James, James Bond

«I see, and how are we getting there in real life ?

«The bus

«Bus ?

«Sea bus

«Great

«And load you camera

They get out of the train, buys a map at the station and do their calm walk down to the water bus station and buy some tickets. They steps out the pier and waits for the next arriving boat. They are looking around, it is just like arriving a new planet. However much they have looked at pictures, the view of the city that is surrounded by canals, marble houses down to the water, mostly white, with a touch of gray, that mirror them self into the green water that is flowing calm, carrying boat in different shapes. The smell of the seawater is in the air, and is completing the atmosphere.

A water bus arrives and they get into the boat, together with their bags, and a lot of people that also, is smiling in this sunny day. Jack makes a lot of photos during the short trip, to their hotel. At the second stop, they get out of the boat and walk into their new place of living for a couple of nights. The hotel is like other hotels, but smaller, space in Venice is not what they got most of, but the positive effect is that they have an intimate atmosphere. Tiny lanes, in Italian style, like other villages that remains on the top of small mountains in this country. There are tiny canals to, and a large canal that looks like an giant S at the map, like an giant calm warm wave.

They agreed to go for a walk after they checked into the hotel. Venice is a famous city, and there are lot of things to see. Jack asks

«Do you know why Maria want you to go here

«Not really, you know women they talk in codes that we don't understand.

«Yes

«Well we should just do as the other people do here

«Walk hand in hand

«Very funny, but no thanks, thanks of asking. Carl laughs

«Lets find out what is to see in this city

«I got some few landmarks on my list

«And what is that ?

«The famous bridge, that one with roof that goes over the main canal, the big piazza and a palace.

«Nice, lets walk

«And as the common bad habit of the nature of human, we need to eat.

«Yes, a really bad habit, Jack laughs

«Famous bridge here we come.

They walk out of the hotel and into the main street, if it is possible to call it that, but the street is surrounded by shops in different styles. There are a lot of art shops. Jack stops at some of them and Carl follows.

«Are you going to buy something?, asks Carl

«Don't think so, these paintings is more like souvenirs from this city. Maybe I am able to get better pictures with my camera, because these pictures have no soul.

«How?

«In old days, they made painting like we do today in photos, just a copy of the picture of how it looked, new art is telling something.

«So if you would by a painting, how would it look like ?

«I don't know, maybe I will buy a book with some paintings, just a memory of this city.

«That is maybe a great memory

«Yes, it is.

They walk for a while looking around, and reach the bridge, which is amazing. Marble brick covers the whole bridge from bottom at the green water up to the blue sky. There are windows in a roman style, bows with straight walls. Underneath the bridge the are many gondolas traveling slowly in the sun, with strong gondoliers with black trousers and striped tops, making them into their way to their destiny. Some of them are carrying couples in love and some are having families. Jack makes some pictures and then they walk into some small streets, finding them a nice small restaurant, with a pleasant environment, with small tablets, checker work clots in the colors red and white and a candle one each table. They order spaghetti with clams, in well odorous garlic and some red wine of the house, together with some tomato salad.

«It seems that you are loosing weight, Carl

«Thanks, Italian food is nice

«And healthy

«Maybe, maybe I can made it to a habit

«Maria would like that habit

«Yeah, she talks about is sometimes, Carl laughs.

«Never too late, Jacks says with a smile

«Lets walk to the Piazza San Marco after this dinner

«Nice, how do you think about Venice?

«It seems nice, but it is different than what I thought about it when I ordered the trip.

«Better or worse ?

«Different

«How

«Maybe I don't know yet, it is difficult to put words it. Have to get some more feelings about it. Pictures don't have smell and people that are living.

They finish up the dinner, in no rush, watching people that walks slowly outside the restaurant. They walk threw the streets, in their way to the piazza, crossing many small marble bridges and narrow streets. They stops at some of these bridges and are looking at boat a and gondolas that is traveling, in these small narrow canals. The sound is reflection in the walls and these windows covered by windows shutter in many different colors. Some of them have new Painting, making telling that the residents are living in the house, there are some old ones to. The reach the magnetically piazza, large as a stadium, with buildings around the place. A lot of tables are in front of the restaurants, and there are small orchestras playing in traditional music like Vivaldi. Carl and Jack is stopping with a amazed look when they enters the piazza.

«Lets get a table, order some espresso and some water, says Carl

«Good idea, this look is to be placed into our minds for a long, long, time.

The piazza is covered with light. The roman bows that surrounds the place, is lightened up making the piazza romantic. There are some couples dancing to the music. They dance with high energy and is connecting their eyes to each other, to read their movements and having what unseen connection between them. Jack makes some pictures, but he shakes his head, and knows that the evening in coming into the piazza, even if the full moon tried to lighten up the blue sky that is turning darker and darker. Carl is looking at the people and says

«All these happy people makes me, happy

«Nice to hear, makes me happy to

«Lets stay for a while, do you see the watch at that building

«Yes, what about it

«It got no, indicators, just showing a happy sun.

«Yeah, you are right

«Another thing, I wish to mention is about this city

«Yes?

«When we walked between these narrow canals, I realized something, this city is drowning slowly

«How?

«Well, the water is up to edge of the bridges, it is full moon

«Yes

«If the water rises in the couple of years, you know pollution, North pole and Greenland is melting, this city will disappear.

«That will be horrible

«Yes, they are working very hard to stop, these buildings from falling apart already, did you notice

«No

«In some of there narrow streets, there was a lot of building material. They really try heard to save this city

«That is nice, Venice is a dream of many people around the world

«Yes, it is

«Maybe that was the reason Maria wanted you to go to this place, write about it and telling the world to stop the pollution.

«Good point, my friend, I will write it up in my mind

«Do that Carl, let us enjoy this evening, try to put those sad thoughts

into the memory bank.

«Right, thanks my friend

«Positive thoughts is very important, focus on what is best

«Maybe that

«Well I believe that positive thoughts are in every human, and these should be brought up to their best, that makes people shine.

«You are clever, thanks

They are relaxing in the mood of the evening atmosphere, that makes this piazza shine to the end of the evening. They return to the hotel, walking happy passing the small bridges and quite canals, and agree to meet at the breakfast table. As in Milan, the name fast is the right name there to. Espresso in small cups and some sugar on white bread, maybe it is a sign that breakfast is not the most important meal of the day.

«So what is the plan for today, Carl ?

«I just thought of walking around, looking, finding something, big some gold, maybe find a treasure

«I just think I will pass that one

«Do you have any other suggestion ?

«I was thinking about going to and art exhibition, there are lot of them.

«Nice, I will join you

«I don't think so, my experience from Milan was that you are killing the art.

«Sorry about that, maybe we should be separate today

«Thanks, was afraid to ask

«Just like me, when I was young

«You ?

«You know, Maria! Carl says with a discreet voice

«Ohh, yeah, Jack laughs

«Lets meet later today

«Yes, at dinner time 8 pm ?

«That is to early let us make it 8.04 pm

«That is nice, and I am happy to know that I going alone

«Funny, very funny, Carl laughs

Jack walks to some of the exhibitions in the city, drops into some of them, and at the pier at the end of the city, there is a large exhibition in a park, with stands from many counties. He walks to the gate, and there are an ally with large trees and sounds of cicadas making him feel that he is in a different place that Venice. There are a lot of halls with art, modern art. He walks into them, to see what each country is representing. The first two halls are with paintings, structure painting, making them with depth. Painting that almost live. In the next hall they are showing a film from Afghanistan, a film maker has followed some routes threw the country, mostly representing the real life of the country, the poor and that war damages. He watches the whole movie, only disturbed by some girls, more interested in their hair, than the movie. In the next hall he really start to wonder, they seems just to place some things abound in the rooms. He looks at the other people, to see if they are understanding what the artist is telling. They looks like questions too, so he passed fast to several halls with similar art. Then he gets into a hall, where a child is playing in the art. There are a lot of steel wires in the room, he doesn't understand the art, but the kid that is playing is making him happy. He walks into the café for a short lunch, and buys some food, the menu is represented with ecological food. He sits down and smiles and is thinking that he really enjoy this art exhibition, and he is very impressed, because there are lot of art about the well being of earth and how humans act to each other.

After the lunch he walks to the rest of the halls, some of them are really having fun art too, and the final hall is the American exhibition., showing a doll in a swimming pool, with liqueur bottles and cigarettes floating in the water. Well typical American style, just how we are, he thinks and maybe I should talk Italian rest of the day.

He walks back to the pier and the mood of the sunset is catching him . The blue sunny sky turns into red. He walks back to the hotel with his camera that has been his friend of the day, happily catches a lot of pictures. Maybe the galleria to Maria is interested in my pictures, but he is not shore about if they are good enough. Only the future will show, he is happy anyway to catch a lot of good memories.

Carl walks around, he has got his PC with him, just in case he gets a inspiration of writing something. The heat is still high, so writing is difficult, but when he sits down and looks around he get some ideas, and then there are some words longing from going from his mind into the keyboard. Sometimes, they run fast, sometimes the keys is like glue. Carl walks to an piazza called Campo Steffano, not far from the the bridge Porte Accademia, that crosses the great canal Grande, find him a nice place to sit. He has a view to a church tower, that is looking like the Pisa tower, leaning to one side. There are several tower like this in the city, leaning to one side. Carl thinks, why go to Pisa when we got it all here. There are several other buildings around in the piazza, making it into a nice Italian atmosphere. He picks up his PC and starts to write, and he is very happy with the writing. At the table beside, there is a man sitting doing some writing to.

«Hey, are you a writer, Carl asks kindly

«Yes, he says and is looking up to see who is talking

«I am Carl, planning to be a writer too

«I am William, and is writing song lyrics, the man says

«Songs?

«Song lyric writer

«Ohh, isn't that hard

«Well, maybe, it makes me a living

«Great, do you sing your self

«No

«I was thinking about to write a book, but I am not quite shore about what, yet. I am traveling with a friend.

«That is hard work to write a book

«Yes, I was a magazine write before, so writing is not the problem

«That is great

«Yes, but the magazine was shut down, bad time for money

«Yes, there have always been hard time, working hard is the only way back

«I have tried different things in my life, and my wife is supporting me of writing

«Great, what does she do ?

«She is running a gallery

«That is nice

«What are you writing on ?

«I have not decided yet, but maybe it is a start of and modern musical, who knows how the future is looking

«It is a open book, Carl laughs, can I see what you are writing on ?
«Yes, it is called take me to Venezia

Take me to Venezia, Walk me to Venezia
I will tell you grazie, please take me to Venezia

To Venezia, To Venezia

Bridges in art, Bridges in poetry
Canals in green, Canals in shine
People in happiness, People in love
People in happy mode, People in lucky mode

Hold my hand in Venezia, I will tell you Grazia
I will take you the Opera, then I will take you to a piazza
I will take you to a palace, then I will take you to a boat
I will make you shine, then I will make you princess
I will make you wonderful queen

Hold my hand in Venezia, I will show you the moonlight
I will hear your dreams, I will wear your thoughts
I will care your thoughts

In Venezia, In Venezia, In Venezia, In Venezia
Let our love grow, Let our love grow, Let our love grow
Your are the shining one, My heart is really gone
Let our lights show, Let our love grow

Let the wind blow, Let our passion show

Let our souls glow, Let our love grow
Let our love grow, Let our love grow, Let our love grow
Let the light flow, Let the light grow, Let the light throw
Let the light show

Let me see your eyes, Let me see your ties, Let me see your soul,
Let me see your goals, Let me into your heart, Let me into your chart
Let me into your start, Let me be your part

Let our love grow, Let our love grow, Let our love show,
Let our love flow, Angels in love, True love they will show, Love that only grows, Like a warm wind it will flows

They are calm like the sea, Their love is free
That is what we can see, Harmony is really free
Angels in love, Angels in love, Angels in love, Angels in love
Light as the wind, Love they will find, Wings like feather,
Dancing in any weather

Colors of white, They are so bright, Angels can fight,
Do they every night, Children they care, Children they wear, Children they bear, Children they hear

They travel in the night, In the crystal star light,
They tell us to have clear sight
That is right, doing a human fight
Angels in love, Angels in love, True love they show,
Let our love grow, Let our love grow, Let our love grow
Your are the shining one, My heart is really gone, Let our lights show,

Let our love grow, Let the wind blow, Let our passion show,
Let our souls glow, Let our love grow

Let the light flow, Let the light grow, Let the light throw,
Let the light show, Let me see your eyes, Let me see your ties,
Let me see your soul, Let me see your goals

Let me into your heart, Let me into your chart
Let me into your start, Let me into your part
I will try to be romantic, I will try to be fantastic
Maybe I am elastic, Maybe I am drastic

Let me play a melody, Let me play in harmony
Let me play in fantasy, Let me paint your fantasy
Let me color your fantasy, Let me hear your fantasy

Let me wear fashion, Let me wear passion
Let me sing my song, Let it stay ever long
Let me dance you, Let me fantasy you
Let me learn you, Let me wear you

Let me love you, Let me love you
Let me love you

«Wow, that was really really great says Carl, you are like William Shakespeare.

«Thanks, he smiles and says, so you are able to read poetry

«Yes, guess so, Carl says and pulls his shoulders upwards. Carl starts to think and is asking

«Maybe you can help me, learn me

«In what ?

«Help write a poem, my wife loves them

«Guess so, do you have any keywords

«Yes

Carl walk up to William, and starts to write down some keywords. William looks at them and makes some suggestions out of words, and after not to long, just the time of that Carl has ordered some pizza to them both, they have been working together to get a poem.

«Thanks

«Just a pleasure, working together is really nice, writing is a lonely thing, just working in your mind

«Shore about that

«I miss the people back at my old work, because that was maybe the best part.

«Yes. Know about that, I am joining some Internet communities, but that is virtual people, we need real people

«Agree, when I get back, I will rejoin my buddies at the matches

«That is nice, I am kind of looking for a wife, but also want to be free. It is not easy to find kind ladies these days.

«With your lyrics, I guess that you are finding a lot of them.

«The performers are the people who gets the credit, the fame credit., anyway it is how the word is spoken that gives the power. In one way I wish I was like that, writers don't go to the cool parties, William says and smiles

«Maybe I am the luckies man in the world, because I got a wife that supports me all the way, and what we wrote together is my gift to her

«And remember to write, to my lovely wife, in the first section, he laughs, and you seems to miss her

«Yes, I do, being in Venice without her gives me a strange feeling, just like I am half.

«Maybe, I don't think I have been I love with anyone before, true love

«Maybe you can ask the stars.

«How ?

«I don't know, maybe my wife knows, here is my contact information, maybe me can come and visit me if you would like

«Great, you seems to be a very nice man.

«Maybe we can write something more together, my friend tells me I am a funny man, so maybe we can write some funny poetry

«Great

«I should be going, because this is my last day, many things to watch.

«We will keep in touch

«Thanks, hope so

«Good luck with your book

«Thanks you to with your.......words

Carl walks away after they have finished up the meal, he walks in the direction of the Piazza San Marco, he is not quite shore about where he walking, because Jack has got the map. He follows the stream of the people. After passing some canals and bridges, he stops and he feels that he got lost, so he stops and is looking carefully around. People seems to have changed, so he feels that he is not in the mainstream anymore. He looks at he buildings and tries some of the narrow streets to find the way back. He stops in frond of a building and reads the sign theater de comedia. He looks at the building for a long time, and then he says to him self. Well maybe this is one of my signs of the day, maybe I am going to write something funny, and gets a good feeling.

He returns and just walks away just follows what is right, suddenly he is on track again and reaches the great piazza. He walks out to the canal Grande and stops at the statue in front of the construction of the magical basilica. He is looking at the old clock tower, to get the time, and he remember his observation of yesterday. The clock has only astrological symbols. He thinks this day is really strange, just like that I am getting a lot of signs. He turns around and walks to the canal there is a large statue in front of him, and he wonders about it, because it has a lion with wings. He thinks that one is strange, and walks into a bookstore to find a book about Venice. He smiles to him self when he walks out of the store, in the memory of that he is copying what Jack does, and thinks that he is a good teacher and a great friend. He walks down to the water and starts to read, but he doesn't find anything what the water lion really is. He decide to walk into somewhere they got an Internet connection, so that he can connect and find some information about it.

He walks in the direction back to his hotel, and finds a nice restaurant, that has connection. He order a beer, a Carlsberg, to much wine with Jack, and connection to the net, and starts to tap into his wonder toy. In his thoughts, he is saying, research is funny and makes me happy, maybe Maria was right, and becoming myself. He doesn't find any information about it, but he is able to find something that the city symbol is maybe after that someone stole the body of St. Mark, from Alexandria to Venice. It is also mentioned that he was the man who carried the water to Jesus in the last supper, painted by Leonardo da Vinci. That was strange, because he just thinks that the death of Jesus was an act. Maybe it is that Jesus walked to Alexandria, who knows, there was a great library there in old times. Well that is not his business to find out, so he continues his search, and he finds something in *Mesopotamian mythology* that has something about winged bulls and lions. It is a bull man helps people fight evil and chaos. Carl finds this interesting and continue to read about this Shanash. He holds the gates of dawn open for the sun god Shamash and supports the sun disc. He searches what the the sun disc is and realized, that the clock tower was a sun disc, that was his sign. He gets really interested and searches that sun disc is used in Mesopotamian, Egyptian and Maya culture. All these cultures died out in someway of some reasons, humans still exists. He doesn't quite understand, the relationship, but anyhow, steeling is a bad thing. He starts to read the book again instead and find out that the winged lion at the clock tower is holding a book, and that is symbol of peace.

He walks back to the hotel, tiered in his mind, of all the information, to get some rest before he joins Jack to have some dinner.

They meet at the lobby of the hotel at the agreeable time, and walks together out to the pier of the city, passing the basilica and statue the winged lion outside Ducal Palace. They find them an restaurant with the view of the ocean. In the walk they talk about what they have been doing.

Self knowledge is when we understand

The wise dome of knowledge land

Our selves and are in true love

As the stars will show

Within our souls

Peace is our goals

Traveling home

The next day Carl wakes up early in the morning, and he gets dressed and walks outside the hotel to watch the sunrise. The city seems to be sleeping, but there are some people doing some walks at the piers. He walks in the direction of the sun. The color of the sun is in between red and yellow. The sky is clear and blue, and there is a cold breeze in the air, that makes him chilling down from the hot night that has hot and covered his body with sweat.. When he reaches the pier, he walk out to the edge and look down into the water. The smell of the water is nice and fresh, and there are several small fish hunting for food. He looks at them, and is wondering if they have feelings, do they know anything about the world, or are they just hunting around for something to eat and trying not to be eaten themselves. There are several fishermen out on the pier. They have fishing rods and seems to be catching small fish, maybe for dinner to their families. There is a boy walking together with his father not far away. The boy runs around looking and wonders about what he finds. The boy is in the age of willing to learning about everything. He stops and looks at the fishermen for some seconds and walks up to his father, and asks.

«Can we fish too ? With a voice that is pleasant and very asking

«Do you remember last time we did that ? The father says with a smile, and a face telling him that he really remembers the last one.

«Nope! He says and nods with his head

The father looks at him, into his eyes for some seconds, after some seconds he makes a smile and says to him

«Let me remind you about the story, let us sit down her at the pier, and then you can look at the fishermen at the same time.

«Yes, dad, he says and walks to the edge of the pier where he has a good view of the fishermen and made space to his father, besides him.

Carl has as usual long ears and wants to hear this story too, so he stops and find himself a nice place to sit on a bench, that is just behind them. He smiles happy to him self about this bench, just like that the boy wanted to him to hear the story.

The father makes him comfortable, and uses some time to watch the calm water, that has small waves that is making the sunbeam making the water into blinking magical light. Like holding a diamond up to the light and look at the light that is broken into several magic lights in the prism of a diamond.

The father tells a story about that he caught a fish, and his son run to him and started to play with it, just like a toy. He tried to stop him, but he didn't stop before he told him that the fish was hurting, so they better kill it quickly like fishermen and hunters do when they have a catch. The son smiles, and remembers, he is looking like that he was going to test his father if he remembered. The boy gets up on his feet and is running to the other fishermen instead.

Carl walk back to the hotel and is getting ready of the return. Getting his bag and stuff. He calls Jack and asks

«Ready ?

«Yes, I am, Jack says in the phone.

«Ready for checkout then.

«Yes, see you.

After the checkout, they walk back to the train station, to get back to the airport.

Teaching is when we learning

The truth we are wearing

The truth about the earth in universe

In great love to humans

2
2

Home coming

After they got their bags, they got into a taxi. They where looking forward to get back, back to their normal life. The vacation, or maybe more like a study, had been very funny and exiting. Jack was looking forward to get back to work and spend some time together with his child. He missed her very much and all the people at his work.

It was almost like coming back from another planet, because all the things that they had seen and talked about was just like a dream. They   need to to get back on the ground, make a firm grip at their life. They didn't speak much in the taxi, but, when it turned up in front of the apartment of Maria and Carl, they talked about that the trip has been very exiting, and maybe they will go on another trip later, a trip of hunting of treasures. Jack was happy to help Carl and they have become great friends. Knowing each other, in a different way, than they was able to is they just had meet in the regular way, in this city.

Friendship is when we give our souls

To other humans in great love

Without requiring anything in return

Not making a heartburn

Carl stepped out of the taxi, and got his bag, and stepped back to Jack, and handed out his hand.

«Thanks, my friend. Trip was really exiting, I have learned a lot about life, and you my friend. Take care, and see you later

«Take care, and give a hug to Maria from me

«I'll do

He walk into the hall and gets up to the apartment, and opens the door and shouts gently

«Hello, angel, are you home

«Yes, I am, she answers with a happy voice, almost singing in happiness

«Great, he says. He can feel that aura, the good aura of the apartment, coming deep into his soul, and fills him with happiness, and says

«I have just been in the Bermuda triangle, but more like Italian triangle. I am just going to tell you, later

«What ?

«I have picked up a lot of codes, secret codes

«Tell me ? She answers, with and interested voice

«Nice, I just got back, but I will write you about it

«What ?

«A book, a book with many words and some thoughts

«Thanks, best home coming gift, I ever got, in my life.

«Any how, he laughs with a sky voice, you are my best gift in my life, he says and walks to her and takes her gently and kindly into his arms look her deeply in her eyes, and smells her neck, before a kiss with passion makes them into one again.

She looks at him and smiles, a smile with true love. Carl replies with

«Next trip, I want to go with you, traveling in love, true love. I have written something to you as a small gift.

«What is that ? She smiles and looks at him, with some excitement.

Carl walks back to his bag that is in the hall, and picks up his new PC and makes it alive. He walks back to her and shows the screen. She starts to read, and smiles, makes a stop and says to him, please read it to me, my love.

The first one is a song and the other two is a short stories written like performed by William Shakespeare and written by Franic Beacon. The last one is a great code maker too.

Ohhh Maria

You soul is a shine, please let us dine
Would that be fine, I will bring some Tuscan wine
Gentleman as maybe I am, I am just not a glam
Style hope I got, my feelings are very hot

Let us go to Lombardia, where the lake meets the mountain
People really shine, fashion are making them very fine

Ooooh Maria, Ooooh Maria
Ooooh Maria, Ooooh Maria

The white shining Angel,
Like the sparkling bubble of the angel
Poems I will write, Every lovely night
My feelings are not on fight,
That is a true human right

You are like a star, making me totally far
You are a singing star, riding you crystal car

Ooooh Maria, Ooooh Maria, Ooooh Maria Magdalena, Magdalena

Passion

We talk in many words, We look in many directions
We hear in many sounds, We move in many ways
We taste in many flavors, We smell in many odors

Passion is what we seek, into our glowing cheek
Every day in every week, that makes our love unique
Passion search the cousin of life, like a magic heart steeling thief
Love we want to be in our life, even if it breaks out hearts with a knife

Hidden passion, seeking passion, growing passion, wonderful passion

Passion will let the years grow, love is a long walking road
Understandings we cannot throw, words of communication is the flow
Love of words make us into pride ladies and lords

Passion reaches the understanding heart
Passion we cannot buy at any mart
Passion is starting in our own heart
Passion is a long walking chart

Hidden passion, seeking passion, growing passion, wonderful passion

seek
thief
steeling
smell
hear
Every
cousin
directions
hearts
flavors
make
pride
chart
walking
words
magic
understanding
search
like
heart
reaches
love
long
Understandings
Love
ladies
life
road
years
seeking
unique
makes
want
day
Passion
wonderful
starting
look
many
odors
talk
glowing
Hidden
check
throw
communication
knife
flow
growing
ways
week
grow
taste

Another universe

The planet

Far far away in a another universe
Where they sing in several verse
There is a wonderful beauty planet
and a wonderful pleasant climate

It has endless fields of straws
Like them we got in our vases
Straws that waves gently in the wind
A wind that feels gently to the skin

The air is covered with smells of flowers
Into their minds it everyday showers
Flowers that wave like fields of wheats
White flowers that smells like sweets

Sweets that is melting on their tongue
Making the souls having a wonderful song
Into the amazing taste where it belongs
Their senses are wonderful strong

The people live in complete harmony
Like a amazing colorful symphony
Flowing in the waves of colorful fields
Making their hearts free of our shields

The planet is surrounded by several moons
Moons that is visible nights and afternoons
They are protecting the wonderful planet
From hitting dangerous traveling comets

The moons are making a magic caring force
Power of the light is their strong force
That is the also the planets strong source
Traveling around and around in its course

The sky is looking blue with gliding clouds
White clouds traveling together in crowds
Making showers to the almost endless fields
Fields growing green creating air that not yields

In the ends of these fields there are mountains
Reaching up to the blue sky like fountains
Having a caring wind shield as a function
Strong solar storms making winds common

amours
Millions
mystic
great
Daylight
Emotions
faces
Feelings
tzar's
Love
magical
warming
show
travel
loan
human
light
Making
like
true
verse
heart
Angels
almost
casual
commerce
delight
moonlight
smilling
sky
old
rices
stars
alright
serial
goes
going
arrow
mysterious
Venus
universe
bow
hearts
sun
stars
slight
glow
throw
Pride
actual
Maybe
shining
moon
Like

The planet town

In the other end there is a small town
That is under the glass bow it is shown
The glass bow is shield fence to the ground
A fortress that is not making it grown

The glass fortress is in a island in a lake
Fresh water is needed as an intake
Making the town living awake
Water is their important sake

Their care much about the fresh lake
The people of the town done in handshake
Pollution to source of living they not break
That could make their living a mistake

Inside the town there are several houses
Looking like large cubes of white sugar
Making the whole town look like a sculpture
Looking like a pyramid of a new culture

Houses are put together making circles
Looking like towers of old castles
Reminding of stones like white marble
With views of the lake and the coastal

The coastal is covered with white sand
As long as the eye can see far land
This is the planets great known brand
This was the best planet when they scanned

The people of the planet is earthly kind
Kindest hearts in their universe to find
Smiling faces make visitors into shine
Rulers of the planet have peace in mind

Peace is their mission in their universe
Force and power is not what they coerce
They are listening careful in any converse
Using diplomacy before it gets worse

Mission

They receive a message from another universe
From a planet where they sing in reverse
The message is in words of several verse
Message is that a comet is hitting their course

The management of the peace planet
Study the message to every small digit
Reading that the comet is a danger rocket
That the strange planet is the real target

They investigate and calculate the future hit
They have to be in action very quick
They have to pick best warriors in fit
This mission they never can quit

They walk threw their list of warriors
Talking to the wise hologram preacher
That is also their wise digital teacher
They make a plan into their minds deeper

A rescue mission is made to the planet
Several plans are made in to a packet
Sending the packet to warriors jacket
Warriors waiting in the field to transit

A number of four warriors collect into a team
They are brave and making into a shine
Working hard making them proud and fine
That is the message of the warriors theme

Warriors are working in couples like partners
To make the ever best know peace keepers
The warriors names Cronus and Rhea
Oceanus and Tethys was at the best lists

They was to enter the best rescue ships
Their names was a everybody's lips
They was trusted to enter the danger trips
That was on the peace planet new lists

A mission was planned come to action
Warriors was smiling to get some reaction
The great rescue mission was in traction
The mission was a long wanted fiction

Travel

They travel in amazing light of speed
Fuel they used power of light to feed
The power of the sun was their need
That is how they use the light to seed

They had several flying rocks to fight
Advanced technology was their insight
Every fight they managed in the light
Knowledge they uses to do the right

The ships Nippur and Eridu traveled elegant
Dancing smooth and not like an elephant
Traveling in sound of the universe quite silent
Warriors was in their true happy segment

The both ships had to do several rolls
Heading to their final destination goals
Maneuvers away from many black holes
Force of the light was in their souls

They passed several space dragons
Sleeping in their bed like wagons
Cottons dreams was their commons
Fighting cute dragons is not their missions

Sometimes they uses power of magic
That is some of their training basic
This makes these warriors fantastic
Not like the creatures of the classic

These warriors have weapons of mystic
Gliding weapons like the power of lyric
Weapons made of magic power karmic
Moving faster than any known drumstick

The planet of the mission in fiction
It was in their eyes of the horizon
The long travel to the planet Abzu
Was their coming to their minds true

Landing outside their strong pantheon
Was a good feeling made them strong
They could hear the sounds of song
The rescue message was not wrong

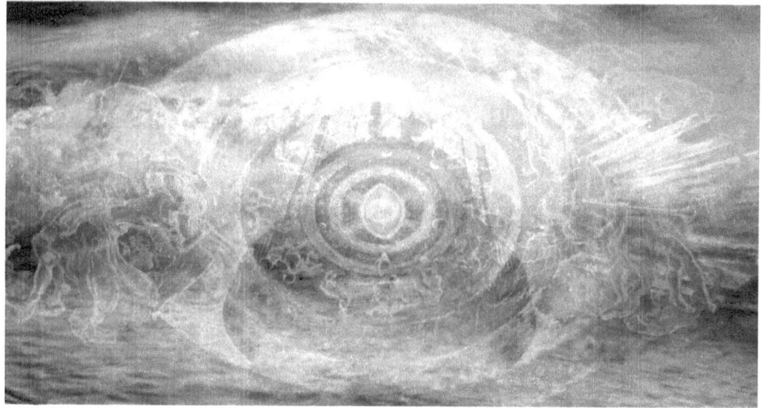

People of the planet

People of the arriving planet they welcome
They know where these warriors are from
New hopes in their hearts are grown
Their kindness in their grown spirit now

The warriors enters the door by guardians *lions*
That is strong guardians like tall strong canyons
They are watching the entering visitors like *twins*
Ready to make fighting like wild hurricanes

They are helped threw the doors by *maidens*
Into a great grand hall that wide broadens
and a large roof reminding of turned *scales*
The atmosphere of the room full of tales

They are offered fresh *water* as drink
They call a *bearer* to make their link
While they are watching a *fish* in a sink
That will make their heads clear to think

The warriors know the people want action
The care about their planet like a *scorpion*
This mission has to be fast, not like a *crab*
There are no time for a long sky lab

The people has named the comet *Archer*
A dark traveling stone that is not a charmer
That is going to be a big crash in flame fire
That is why they want these warriors of hire

The warrior has a magic weapon called the *Bull*
Powerful to move the comet with a *ram* pull
That is cleaver and brave as the old *goat*
That is solution how to reach their goal

This weapon will *Shake* the loaded atmo*sphere*
Making this *universe* out of its fear
That is made totally understandably clear
To the understandable people that will hear

WARRIORS
LIKE
STRONG
ACTION
PLANET
PEOPLE
WEAPON
ATMOSPHERE

Execution

Into the blue sky brave warriors fly
To give the rescue mission successful try
The threating planet they will set free
To their target soon they will be

First they had to round a moon called Galileo
These days it is a nice shining fellow
Making fun in the shine of the yellow
In the old times, men of towers don't follow

Warriors travel in their ships made of *science*
Their knowledge is made up of learning valiance
Their great mission becoming shorting distance
This mission will give them great prudence

That is just a *psychological* visible fact
Their mission made them hurry react
From their home peace planet contact
They have a peace mission contract

Then they rounded the next moon call Horus
That make the rest of the trip in chorus
Into the sky that was blue and cloudless
and felt like that it is ever boundless

Party

Coming back to the strange planet
Congratulations music was out of basket
They played a song called Alexandria
Written by a princess call Cleopatra

She had use inspiration of the muses
Lost in long time hidden treasures
This is the new song of the future
Written in a great large boulder

She replaced the old bad song
called Caesar from a rain tower
That one was lost in a long shower
killed all the smells of the flower

They offered the warriors gold
They say they wanted to fold
Their happiness is to be bold
True warriors souls are not sold

Peace and happiness is their gold
That is what the preacher has told
Their peace planet has its household
Even if their planet it is not old

They answered yes to champaign
This was a great peace campaign
Strange planet had nothing to complain
They where getting rid of the pain

A toast of glass in the victory
belongs to the written history
Warriors had no hidden glory
They danced to sound of boogie

Back to the ships they after went
After the long lasting party event
Waiting for a new message sent
That is the warriors true present

They traveled back in reverse
To their own peace universe
where they in calm peace coherence
That is what told in this last verse

Warrior of the light

The warrior of the light, Is able to do his fight
To archive what is right
The warrior of the light, Is maybe clever and bright
Powerful to do whats right

The warrior of the light, Never goes to a gunfight
Some words is what he is going to write
The warrior of the light, Is looking into the candle light
With his hands he is going to write

The warrior of the light, He has the clear sight
He follows the starlight
The warrior of the light, Is doing his word fight
Writing in the moonlight

The warrior of the light, Writes his words in the night
In the northern light, He wants every body
To be safe in the night
The warrior of the light, Feels what is right
His heart doesn't have to fight

The warrior of the light, Is doing feelings alright
Because peace is in his sight

Discovering America

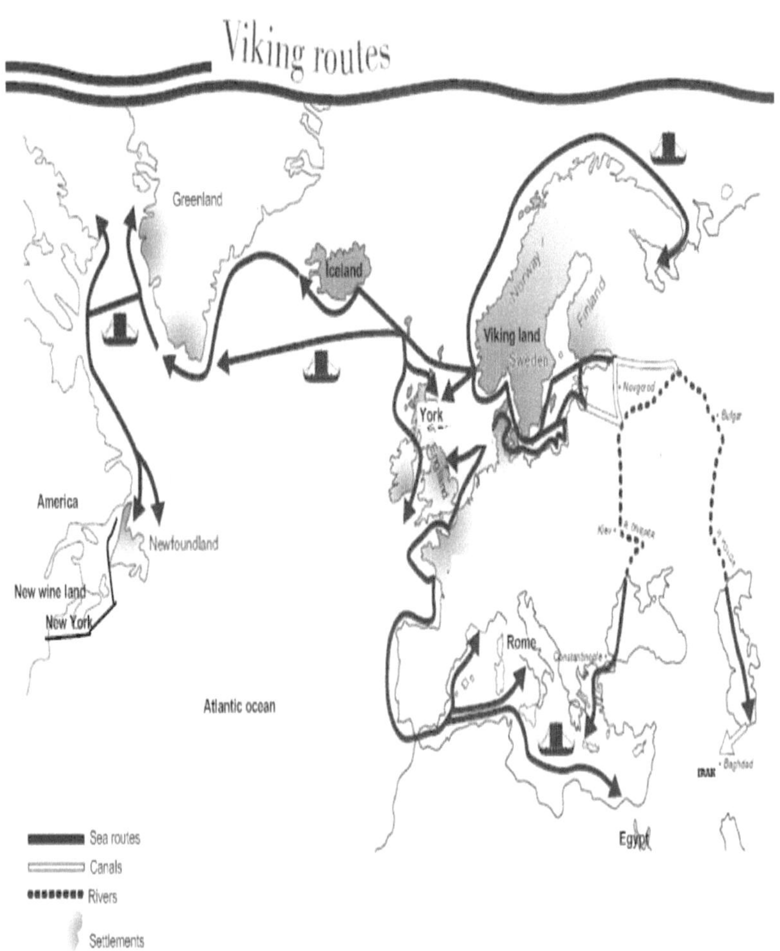

A viking boy

Several of hundreds of years
Before we learned about angel feathers
There was a viking boy, playing with his toy
Listening to stories, that adults told
His toy he could fold, because his soul was sold

He was sitting by the fire
These stories was not told by a liar
It was stories about a far land
Far far away from this golden sand
Behind the large mountains
And wonderful canyons

There was no frightening dragons
But about horses and wagons
There was gold and diamonds
Princesses waiting at stations

There was something talking about love
That these adults told, that will grow
The little boy wanted to go, where these warm winds blow
He wanted to be a viking king, where his heart could show
But first he had to sleep and get out of the shadow

The midnight sun, made the thoughts run

Exploring new countries is going to be fun
The next years, he trained with his sword, in his hand
He strike the air, and learned nothing to fair

They asked him for his name
He answered Leif, with no shame
Leif Eiriksson
Son of Eirik, that had stayed for long

He got long golden hair,
and a place with the table, and his own chair
They told him that he was fair
So they wanted him near

They asked him, what do you want to be
He told them he want to be free
They told him if you are going to be a king
You have to learn how to sing

He even learned to sail, he didn't give up when he failed
He learned to navigate by the sun and stars
And that the sea was many deep yards
He learned the nature, that he is going to use in the future.

First travel

He still haven't learn to sing
He needed that to be a king
He wondered where that wisdom could bring
He had to talk to the wise man, with eagle wing

The known wise man
Lived in the north land
He lived far in the north
That was long way from the south

First he had to trade some goods
Some of them came from the woods
He build a large strong boat
Strong as a storm it evens floats

He filled his many barrels
Fish where going to be jewels
He waited for the north wind is his sail
This plan could not fail

South his sails was going
Good luck, was showing
England's castles of York
Is tasting his empty wine cork

Several days he was at travel
Many storms he had to battle
His boat float as a bottle
His knowledge was not at trouble

Several moons later he arrived land
But there was no landing sand
There was only large rocks
He sailed until he found docks

He traded his wooden barrels
Into coins of eden metals
It was a hard battle
Not more than he could struggle

He found a small hostel
He became some hurtful
Nights of wine and music
Was not his heart of lyrics

His destiny was chosen
He was strong as a canyon
He had a big great vision
Far countries was not a fiction

I enjoy the sea

I am sitting at the pier, By the sea I am near
Some birds I can hear, My guitar I want to wear

I am listening to the waves, Looking for what they saves
They wash the earth, Making living worth

I am enjoying the blue blue sea
I am enjoying the green green sea

I am eating some shrimps, And my guitar tickles
I share some wine, Makes my heart fine

A beautiful woman I have at my table
Making my life very stable
She smiles at me, Having eyes like the sea

I am enjoying the blue blue sea
I am enjoying the green green sea

The sea makes me calm, Making my heart warm
I play guitar and sing her a song
All night long

I am enjoying the blue blue sea
I am enjoying the green green sea

Stories

He stayed for several weeks
Fascinating stories was what he seeks
Maybe some secrets they leaks
Something that warms his cheeks

He used different techniques
To get the stories of mystics
It was words of wisdom
From far countries they come

Some where wonderful fairy tales
Strange words like ocean sails
Some where about Romans and Greeks
Some where about Persians and Egyptians

There was gods and hero's
Great giants and small dwarfs
Rich kings and powerful queens
Battling soldiers and steeling thief's

There was shining gold and silver
Sailing ships and stone cliffs
Telling moral and speaking ethics
Amazing magic and cryptic mystics

It was stories of pyramids
Giant graves in triangles
Amazing legendary faros
Ra, Horus and chaos

It was telling stories about
how to live and not without
The great gods like Allah and Buddha
Many coins and harems as a new era

He liked the stories of nymphs
Wonderful music and loving dreams
Amour of love and mystic muses
Beautiful Athene and powerful Zeus

They was talking about the universe
Goddess of the wonderful Gaia
Ouranos, the never ending sky
Golden age of Kronos

It was talking about living in peace
Complete harmony and stability
Well being, every evening
His thoughts where never landing

I am just a viking

I am just a viking, I am just singing
I am just eating, I am just drinking

I am just a viking, I am just hunting
I am just fishing, I am just catching

Just a Viking Just a Viking

I am just a viking, I am just traveling
I am just exploring, I am just finding

I am leaving viking land, I am leaving in my boat
I am leaving the sheep, I am leaving the salmon

I am just a viking, I have just found Rome
I have just found Wine land, I have just found America

Just a Viking
Just a Viking
Just a Viking

Traveling back

He dreamed about beauty
His vision was just like a bounty
He traveled fast on the sea
Just like a humming bee

He fight large waves
Coming from dangerous caves
With his sword, he waves
For several nights and days

He reached his born fjords
Showing off his awards
They played him many chords
Treating him like other lords

He told his wonderful words
and showed his hitting sword
As long as the night records
He wanted more awards

They gave him a large ship
That holds large storming clips
So he could make his dreaming trips
Because kingdom was on his lips
He went back to the ships

That sleeps along with deep cliffs
That was filling up with wooden bricks
He was almost ready to make new trips

He needed a crew, men that he knew
He gave them some tasty brew
They where almost as brand new
They didn't knew, what they where going threw

He took some of the new ships
Strong enough to carry his trips
Commanding words where on his lips
To handle these men on viking ships

The next travel was going north
Because he knows what was is south
He had to learn the singing truth
To carry a worthy king prof

He had to travel through many fjords
Shaking hands with many lords
Traveling horrible many yards
Weather was always like wild cards

Harmony

The sky is blue, and that is true
The sky is free, and let it be

Humans thinks, the world sinks
Minds are free, and let them be

Let the world be free, Wonderful it will be
Let there be harmony, We enjoy charity

We are all one, The true world is not gone
Earth is sharing, We are still learning

Harmony Harmony Harmony

The earth is green, It always have been
Humans really feel, World is like a wheel

Truth is not a deal, It is only what we feel
Birds sings, We do not need all things

We have a smile, We are able to walk miles
In careful hands, Even in desert sands

Harmony, Harmony, Harmony, Harmony

Traveling coast

Traveling along the long coast
needed every man on sharp post
The sun is sometimes strong, maybe roast
Sometimes it feels like making toast

The mountains rises steep up of the ocean
Carrying clouds light as white cotton
Calm sea that mirrors the sky
White birds that smoothly fly

Fog that creeps along with black water
Silence that reminds of a dark camber
Rain that wash sudden rocks
That makes nervous shocks

Winds that tumbles sharp waves
Giving speed into boat sails
Winds that whips waves white
Making sailing men into fights

Ships arrives the north coast
It is time to make a big toast
Glasses and tins fills with brew
Stomachs are filled with tasty stew

It is time to learn to sing
He ask the vise man with eagle wing
He tells him, you need your heart to bring
Then you will wonderful sing

Feel the air, the vibration in the air
Feel the waves, the rolling waves
Feel the mountains, the rolling mountains
Feel the animals, the breeding animals

Feel the threes, the waving threes
Feel the leafs, the falling leafs
Feel the grass, the growing grass
Feel the nature, the living nature

Feel the sun, the heating sun
Feel the moon, the magic moon
Feel the stars, the blinking stars
Feel the world, the human world

Why do I have to sing to be a king ?

You have to be laud, in the crowd
You need to know, when you are fraud
You need to strong, when things to wrong
You need to speak, your own jargons

Freedom

I am sitting on a mountain, It is like a earth fountain
I can feel the earth, We can be rebirth

I can feel the four winds, It is coming to our minds
Into humans it can find, Knowledge we will find

Freedom Freedom Freedom

The change is in the air, Wisdom is very clear
Humans are fair, We all are so dear

We all are living together, Even in bad weather
We feel light as feather, This world is getting better

I love the future, The peaceful future
Living together, The world is getting better

Freedom
Freedom
Freedom

Nature of north

He had to feel the nature
That is only a part of the creature
That is only a our living future
That is only a human capture

He was wondering day and night
His mind was discovering light
He didn't want to wait
He want to walk his faith

He studied the mountains
They where almost like fountains
They where covered with snow
Like pyramids they grow

The mountains where like tones
Made him discover some milestones
They where telling feelings to the bones
Rhythm like that northern mountains own

He studied the wonderful northern light
Colors where dancing in the moonlight
Blue, green and white was the heavens light
Signs to new land was in his sight
He studied the calm sea

It set his soul complete free
It was there he wanted to be
It sounds like fresh honey

Waves was like tones
Sounding like trombones
Sounds that nobody owns
Music is what the soul loans

He studied the seashore stones
Rounded soft surviving cyclones
Smells covered with ocean salt
Like the waves never ending vault

Sounds of the singing nature
Made him lift his heavy anchor
His knowledge was become bolder
Readiness to cut the sea like butter

He was ready to make his tales
Ships where heavy like whales
Food and herbs was under veils
Rosen rot was against fatal fails

Iceland

The next stop was Iceland
That is an volcanic island
In the waters of the Gulf stream
A short visit was his theme

They traveled fast threw the sea
Northern Atlantic they didn't want to be
Tall waves where not making them comfy
Sand fields was what they liked to see

They found several rivers
Fresh water they delivers
That was their savers
It was in their favors

Volcanoes made them scared
Maybe they where not prepared
Thoughts where what they shared
Strong ship men they cared

Steamy waters of lava
Is wonderful in this fauna
Baths in hot water that clean
Caring private welcome hygiene

Finding true love

A wonderful smiling pretty face
Magical wonderful colored eyes
Hitting his exploring ways
In these shining days

Eyes that secret talks
Into the future they walks
Earth and heaven shakes
Marriage in souls it makes

I shape a heart with my hands
Make it glow with my breath
I send it into the universe
Waiting for the next verse

Time is not to walk in reverse
Only knowledge is in this verse
Love is coming to refresh
Future has to ever inverse

Love that I fears, in my soul it wears
My heart and soul have to nurse
True love it not what I fears
Several signs is my guiders

Good aura is like colorful flora
Walls of my heart feels like tundra
Maybe I need a guidance Sherpa
Walking in the land of lava

In hope of reaching heartland
Raising me up of the golden sand
That feels like drowning quicksand
Hope on day to grab a warm hand

Looking ever at the energy of the sun
Until the sky is wonderful red burn
And the moon is lighten in the darken
That is when love will return

That is the true law of love
That only soul mates can show
Maybe amour lifted his bow
Hitting with several arrows in row

She steps in his boat
With love it lighter float
Magical words are in their throat
Love of Iceland is the endnote

Greenland

Next step was giant Greenland
It is a great green farmland
That was the story they where told
Their souls where completely sold

They did only see mountains
With lot of ice it contains
That was not in their frames
Bad stories they blames

They fight polar bears
Made their traveling fears
Into caring warm ears
For several traveling years

They didn't want to he hunters
They felt like bad butchers
They where sorry for these creatures
They where wave fighters

They traveled farer south
That is the known truth
Old settlements are the evidence
Houses of stones is the sentence

Newfoundland

They arrived in the north tip
They grounded finally their ships
New houses was what they rigs
Close to mountains and hills

Finally he found a new land
In these windswept land
They liked staying in the sand
Holding fresh fish in their hand

He finally could raise his crown
As famous kings have shown
New settlements was grown
They was on their own

Nature with large old threes
Is above these cold windy seas
Made them not in the evenings freeze
Fires and stories heat their bodies

This land was just at loan
Many years have been flown
He had found historical milestone
He could sing this own tone

Ode to Newfoundland is still sung

Words are at their tongue
Teaching old and young
That is how the ode is sung

Why the settlement was left
Is a old forgotten theft
Houses are still empty
That is what shown clearly

Maybe they discovered natives
Living their friendly life's
In harmony with the nature
That is their ancient culture

Humans and land cannot be own
Life's are a short time at loan
Who created this wonderful earth
Millions of years from its birth

Earth belongs to every child
We want them to say out of the wild
We want them to have a playing field
Grown ups are their human shield

Home coming

One day, a wonderful day
He was with a strong voice able to say
Wine land is far far away
And he pointed that south east way

I am going another way
My own way, the warm wind way
I am going the south way, the sky way
The warm wind tells me the way

We found new land, newfound land
Far away from viking land
We are just digging in the sand
I want to find a new wine land

Today I am leading the ships away
I don't want to stay, until I get gray
That is the only thing I will say today
Hope you all join me at the survey

They traveled several days
It was sunny days, just like Sundays
They traveled nights and days
Warm winds was in their heart ways
They stopped at a large river

Placed their viking banner
To fill their barrels with water
But some grapes wanted them to get closer

He said, my wisdom, came from a sitcom
Called England's Duke of York
I am going to fill this bottle, under this wine cork
Place my hay fork in the sand, and call it New York

They found wonderful wine grapes
In these wooden landscapes
He placed his bottle in the sand
And called the wine Amour can

Because he did see some red people ran
Maybe they thought he was a space man
But he did not need any more fans
So he just went back and called them Americans

Maybe one day we come back
Maybe we then get some feedback
We are just traveling in peace
Sharing a coin called Nobel prize

Handled with a smiling face!

fine
wonderful
want
Red
taste
flows
sorrounds
fame
shine
red
made
pain
doen't
feel
make
Love
water
wine
dear
destroy
share
fight
fresh
Fields
grapes
shapes
glass
joy
lovely
Calming
deploy
makes
toy
comes
soil
souls
everywehere
white
waves
forget
Wonderful
nothing
glasses
thoughs
Hunting
Wine
caves
Feeling
like
pleasure
fear
drink
head

This is a story (fiction) told in poetry, about discovering North America, Newfoundland, also called Vinland.

The story is told in 85 end rhythm verse, and divided into 9 chapters. The last verse is made in humor, and not based on facts.

There are song lyrics between the chapters. Ode to Newfoundland, is not covered.

The main story is based on some facts, but source us not validated. The main character is about Leif Ericson

Leif Ericson (Old Norse: **Leifr Eiríksson**) (c. 970 – c. 1020) was a Norse explorer who is currently regarded as the first European to land in North America (excluding Greenland) around 500 years before Christopher Columbus. According to the Sagas of Icelanders, he established a Norse settlement at Vinland, which has been tentatively identified with the L'Anse aux Meadows Norse site on the northern tip of the island of Newfoundland in Newfoundland and Labrador, Canada.

Leif and his crew left Markland and again found land, which they named Vinland. They landed and built a small settlement. They found the area pleasant as there were wild grapes and plenty of salmon in the river. The climate was mild, with little frost in the winter and green grass year-round. They remained in the region over the winter.

On the return voyage, Leif rescued an Icelandic castaway named Þórir and his crew — an incident that earned Leif the nickname **Leif the Lucky** .

Research done in the 1950s and 1960s by explorer Helge Ingstad and his wife, archaeologist Anne Stine Ingstad, identified a Norse settlement located at the northern tip of Newfoundland.

Winter

Snow is falling slowly to the ground
White crystals is everywhere found
Like angels have used their magic wand
Having several crystals in their hand

A little girl was looking into the sky
She was looking where angels can fly
She was looking into the night of stars
Lightning stars longer away than eyes sonars

In her hand, she hold her teddy bear
She has a soul that wonderful cares
She was dreaming of amazing stories
Stories that made her thoughts wanders

She was looking for a shotting star
That could travel her thoughts very far
A star that could give her a magic wish
That could serve her dreams on a dish

An caring angel listen to her dreams
The child had wonderful magic themes
The angel used the power of moonbeams
Waking into her wonderful caring dreams

The angel asked her what she likes
The child told a story that earth shakes
It was a story about people in peace
She asked with a caring voice and said please

The angel gave her a singing voice
That was the white angel choice
Able to sing the songs of peace
Until awareness to everybody increase

The girl was wondered about how
The angel from the beam didn't show
She started to look at the crystals of snow
That was making a soft carpet, falling in row

She walked back at her caring home
Thinking about that the angel had shown
Love in her good heart had ever grown
She wanted the angel to be her own

Outside the house of her own
She make an angel in the white snow
She made them smiling several in row
Her wonderful caring heart was at a glow

She looked more at the crystals in the snow
She picked them up and gave them a blow
They where dancing to the ground in a row
Fitting together was what the angel had shown

She could sing with her voice at her own
Sounding like a shining crystal crown
That was the sound she had found
The angel had used the magic wand

In a chorus she now could wonderful sing
Thinking of the angel with the white wing
Singing together would be a wonderful thing
That was the thought of the angel being

The little enlightened girl, trained for her song
Voices of her instrument every day long
Singing to her sweet little teddy bear
That one that she indeed cared

One day she walked into the chorus
The group that was her new fortress
Together they song wonderful words
Going into hearts of adults, as songbirds

Religion is when we try to
Understand the creator of
This universe and humans on earth

Prayer is when are becoming
To our heart asking
Our selves in true love
Humanity we will show
And asking if this is really true
What we really want to do

Good and evil
Is when we are capable
To understand the true words
In our human souls
In true love or not
What have you got ?

Death is when we have completed
Our lives in true love and peace
From being a child, into the wild
To the leaf dead from the three

Walking life (biography)

First I was a small kid, running everywhere, just like a squid
I was at a music kinder garden, because of music didn't frighten
Then my family moved to a villa, I got new friends with no drama
We acted cowboys and Indians, with great Carma., it was a new era

Then I got youth, wondering at a roof, and ended in some Vermouth
My neighbors didn't like my music, my load music, I thought it was fantastic
Is was a rockin roof, and that is the truth, music ruled the roof.
We also had a piano, I didn't know notes, but I played some nice tones

Then I got into some books, a lot of books, I read a whole library
Then I discovered nice girls, with pretty looks, I was shy, I don't know why
Finally I got a girl, with nice curls , I didn't know how, what feelings I could show
I felt stupid like a cow, but music and movements we could show

Then I got old, just like eighteen, I was ready to be a school shine
Computers made me really fine, gettin me off track of crime
I stayed many years, so I got a diploma under my feathers
I even moved to another city, it was a little bit sticky

Just walking life, just walking life

Then I got, really old, family was happiness, I was got told, before I get bold
Job, wife, kids and cars, was glowing in my stars, I didn't see any wars.
I rocket ride jobs, there was some hops, from teacher to a management preacher
I even changed wife, cutting our rings with knifes, lovely kids are still in our life's

Then I got, really really old, but I still have some time to fill
A wanted to be fantastic creative, stopping being boring negative
I started to draw and paint with wonderful colors, even write poetry and photography
I learned about life, life is in cycles, in number of sevens and twenty one.

One day, maybe I can get a new wife, completing my new life
While I am looking at these wonderful stars, that have many answers
I need to use my genes, because to my souls they cleans
Maybe I can write, dance, sing, manage and even act, because genes are facts.
Artists have their feelings intact, and that is positive psychological fact

Just walking life, just walking life
In visible signs, In visible signs

Index

Epilog

The poem, Soul of a woman, in the book is written by an unknown poet, maybe it is created before written form, was the usual form, told in generations.

The facts about Jesus is based on the book, The Jesus Papers written by Michael Baigent 2006. That book has a lot of references. Please ask writer if any questions. Mekka is based on the books of Mohammed and the Koran, I have read the books written by Kader Abdollah.

Hope you had a really fun time. I did when a write this book, it made me free and happy.

I am not telling anyone what to believe, that is not my point of this book. Many of the sign have I seen myself, so they are facts. I made travel to Paris, Milan, Venice and several places in Norway to see and understand what the old poets, maybe felt. I believe in making the best parts of religion, there are many wonderful positive thoughts in every religion. We are all humans on the same planet and same universe. I have use astro.com and *decoz.com* , as my guiders, both for writing this book and personal use.

www.ingramcontent.com/pod-product-compliance
Lightning Source LLC
Chambersburg PA
CBHW030816310726
48980CB00006B/513/J

* 9 7 8 8 2 9 9 8 0 0 9 3 8 *